Standard of Care, a Medical Romance

DL White

Books by DL White

Ebook ISBN: 9798235265233

Print ISBN: 9798996030415

Cover design by DL White, model photo courtesy Depositphotos.

Editing by **AdotKedits**

About Standard of Care, a Medical Romance

A high heat forbidden workplace Medical Romance

Saving him could end her career. He won't let Harper Sutton pay that price.

Dr. Cole Vaughn has spent his career being twice as good for half the recognition. When a patient's family files a complaint that puts his future at Ridgeway Medical Center on the line, he expects to be sacrificed.

What he doesn't expect is Harper Sutton.

As Director of Risk Management, Harper protects patients, enforces standards, and when necessary, ends careers. Dr. Cole Vaughn's investigation should be just another case file. It isn't.

His record is clean, the medicine was sound, and someone powerful has been very careful to make sure none of that matters. The deeper Harper digs, the more dangerous the truth becomes, and the harder it gets to pretend that what's building between them is anything less than what it is.

She holds his career in her hands. He makes her want to tear everything down.

In a system built to protect itself, can two people choose each other without becoming collateral damage?

* * *

Setting: Ridgeway Medical Center, a large metropolitan teaching hospital in a fictional Southern city

Heat Level: 🔥🔥🔥🔥 Open-door. Explicit. Grown & sexy.

Tropes:

- Workplace Romance
- Forced Proximity
- Forbidden Romance (professional ethics conflict)
- He Falls First
- Competence Kink

Content Advisory

This novel contains explicit sexual content, including on-page masturbation and intercourse without protection, strong language, a storyline involving a patient death and the threat of medical litigation. Many scenes take place in a hospital setting. Expect mention of blood, injury, bodily processes.

Themes of grief, professional scrutiny, and hospital politics.

Standard of Care, a Medical Romance

Prologue

The double doors to the ambulance bay at Ridgeway Medical Center swung open with a bang, followed by a pneumatic hiss. A team of paramedics steered a stretcher through, wheels rattling over the threshold.

"Eighty-two-year-old male found unresponsive at a memory care center," the lead paramedic called out. "BP's tanking, heart rate one-twelve. GCS was three at scene."

"Three? Shit." The charge nurse trotted alongside the stretcher. "We've seen him before. Any meds?"

"Metformin, lisinopril, aspirin."

"The family with you?"

"Nah. Brookside said granddaughter was out of town. They left a message."

"Copy that. We'll take it from here."

The patient was a slight, elderly man with paper-thin, sallow skin. His mouth hung open, jaw slack, eyes half-closed. A bag-valve mask sat crooked on his face, fogging with each forced breath.

"On my count," said the nurse. "One, two—"

The team lifted him from the stretcher and lowered him onto the hospital bed. The man weighed maybe a hundred and thirty pounds, but an unconscious body was dead weight. Monitor leads snapped onto the hospital system, EKG pads stuck to his chest, and a blood pressure cuff cinched his arm. A cacophony of beeping and chirping filled the room.

The attending pressed his fingertips into the patient's abdomen. "Distended, rigid, no bowel sounds. Abdomen's full." He straightened then ordered, "Get me a full trauma panel. Type and cross-match for six units. And page Vaughn. We might need the OR."

A nurse drew blood while another started a second IV line. The respiratory therapist leaned over the patient's face, grasping his fingers. "Sir? Can you hear me? Squeeze my hand if you can hear me."

Not even a flicker.

"Let's do an ultrasound."

The resident grabbed the probe and squeezed gel onto the patient's exposed belly, then pressed the transducer against the taut skin as gray shapes appeared on the screen. The probe moved slowly, searching, and then there it was—a column pulsing on the monitor with a dark irregular shadow ballooning outward at its base.

"Ruptured aortic aneurysm," the attending called out.

The trauma bay surged into motion—a nurse barked into the phone, her voice rising just enough to convey urgency; another lunged for the crash cart and yanked open drawers while yet another sprinted toward the hallway to hold the elevator.

"Any info on this gentleman?" the attending asked.

The nurse scrolled the chart on the tablet in her hands, her head shaking slowly. "He's a frequent flier. Family is out of town. The facility left a message that he was being transported here."

"See if you can reach them." He paused and glanced at the monitor. "Tell them we're taking him to surgery."

"Do we need approval—"

"We can't wait. Let's go."

They pushed the bed toward the open bay doors. In less than a minute, the ER was back to its normal hectic flow. The intake note was updated, capturing every note of the patient's care.

Next of kin contacted 13:52. No response, message left. Informed patient admitted to surgery to repair rupture of abdominal aorta.

In the OR, the anesthesiologist worked quickly to insert a tube, secure the airway, and begin the drip of drugs that would keep the patient unconscious while they tried to save his life.

The doors swung open and the surgeon stepped in, mask and goggles on. A surgical tech helped him into his gown and snapped gloves onto his hands before he moved to the table with his eyes on the monitors first, then the patient, taking in the scene.

"What do we know?"

"History of diabetes, hypertension, dementia. Presented with distended abdomen, ultrasound shows a AAA."

"Ruptured aneurysm? We need to get in there."

"Pressure is dropping, doctor," a surgical nurse interrupted. "We don't have any family here. Do you want to hold until—"

The surgeon shook his head. "I'm not scrubbed in to let this man bleed out on my table." He held out a hand. "Scalpel."

The blade cut a long midline incision from sternum to

pelvis. Blood welled up immediately—dark, venous, too much of it. Suction pulled it away but more kept coming.

"Clamps."

The team clamped, packed, suctioned. They tried to find the source of the bleed, to get control, to buy enough time to repair what had ruptured.

Minutes passed and the monitors beeped warnings with alarms going off while the numbers on the screen kept falling.

The surgeon glanced at the clock, then at the monitor, and watched the line that had been jumping with each heartbeat go flat. His hands stilled in the open abdomen as blood pooled faster than suction could clear it, and the monitor showed a heart with nothing left to pump.

"He's too far gone. I'm calling it. Time of death: two twenty-seven."

Gloves came off and the drape stayed in place over the open abdomen, but all work stopped. Someone turned off the alarms.

Dr. Cole Vaughn walked to the corner of the OR, pulled off his cap and gloves, running a palm over his hair as he observed the scene. He stood there for a moment, letting the loss settle.

After over twenty years as a surgeon, every death still lodged in his gut, and this one was no different. The silence, after so much chaos, was heavy.

He stripped off his gown and mask, then pushed through the OR doors into the hallway.

Chapter One

HARPER

The coffee machine hissed and gurgled in the pre-dawn quiet of my kitchen. I yawned, shuffling down the hall toward the heavenly scent wafting through my condo.

I passed the living room, glancing over just to admire it. It was comfy, cozy, made just for me. Everything was in its place because that's how I functioned best—pillows arranged just so, books stacked on the coffee table, a soft blanket folded over the arm of a chair.

My slippers flapped against the heels of my feet as I entered the kitchen. The tablet that lived on the island came to life with a tap. I liked listening to overnight shenanigans while I waited for the coffee to brew.

After one last gurgle from the coffee machine, I filled a thick ceramic mug, added a splash of cream, and took my first sip while watching the city wake up through the sliding glass doors off of the dining room. The city wasn't even awake yet.

This was the time of the day I protected the most. The moment before anyone could demand anything from me, before anything could be spoiled.

The iPad blared reports about some city council meeting and a traffic accident on the interstate; nothing that required my full attention, which was good because my mind was already running through the day ahead.

I had a morning briefing with the rest of the Risk Management and Patient Advocacy teams, I'd scheduled a follow-up on an orthopedic complaint that came in the week before, and I needed to complete an assessment prior to my lunch meeting with the new Director of Surgical Services.

In the pocket of my robe, my phone vibrated. I pulled it out, glanced at the screen, then clicked my tongue softly and slid my finger across the device.

"Did you know most people are still asleep at six in the morning?" I asked, trying and failing to sound stern.

"The early bird gets the worm, I heard." My assistant, Rowan, laughed. "Every morning, you get an attitude about how early I call you and every single morning, you're already up."

"That doesn't mean I want you on my phone."

"Take a few more sips of that bitter ass dark roast that's stripping the lining out of your intestinal tract."

"I'm four sips in, actually. If you're jealous of my custom coffee blend, just say that."

"Ain't nobody jealous of that expensive bean water. My taste buds don't require a second mortgage."

"Don't come for my coffee when you're drinking a

peppermint mocha thing that smells like a Bath & Body Works candle."

"Excuse you! My coffee blend is *delicious*."

"Alright, what's going on?" I asked, already bracing. "You didn't call me before sunrise to debate coffee."

"Yes, I did, but okay. I've been tracking a patient death. The family's starting to ask *questions*."

Noting the inflection, I lowered the volume on the iPad and asked, "What kind of *questions*?"

"The kind they hire a medical negligence law firm to ask. A records request came through Friday afternoon. The review team flagged it."

Patient deaths happened every day at Ridgeway Medical Center. We were the largest hospital in the region, a level one trauma center, the place people came when everything else had failed. When protocols and policies came into question, the Risk Management department got involved.

Most families grieved and moved on. Some asked questions. A few hired lawyers.

"Walk me through it," I said.

The sounds of clicking told me they were already in the file. "Elderly patient brought in unresponsive. ER found a ruptured aneurysm. His condition deteriorated, he was transferred to surgery. Patient died before family arrived."

"Happens," I said. "So, what's the problem?"

"Next of kin is pressed. They're saying they were left out of critical decisions, and no consent was obtained for the interventions."

I frowned. "An imminent situation trumps consent. We aren't going to wait for family to mosey on down to the ER to say yes, we can save a life."

"Normally, yeah. But the patient is a Hart. As in Hart Pavilion, Hart Endowed Chair—"

My eyes slammed shut and I set my mug down with a heavy thunk. "*Fuuuuuuck.*"

"Right." Rowan paused, pushing out a sigh. "Dr. Rice is already in my inbox."

Dr. Elizabeth Rice, Vice President of Risk Management and Patient Advocacy, had never met a problem she couldn't reframe as someone else's fault. She and I had a tenuous relationship. We got along better when she let me do my job. Unfortunately, she was a bit of a helicopter and a micromanager.

"Who was on the case?" I asked.

After a few clicks, Rowan replied, "Aside from the ER team, Dr. Cole Vaughn, trauma surgeon. He's been at RMC about three years. He's as good as they get, from what I hear."

I knew the name, the face, the physique. Dr. Vaughn looked like he'd stepped straight out of central casting of a nighttime medical drama. Mid-forties, dark, moody eyes framed by bushy brows. He had distinguished grays throughout his hair and beard that probably had the nurses doodling his name in their journals at night.

Vaughn didn't seem particularly political. Either he was smart enough not to play games or naive enough to think being good at his job was enough to protect him.

We all learn sometime.

I glanced at the clock. I had time to finish my coffee, get dressed, and arrive at the hospital ready to jump into this case.

"Alright. I'll be there by eight," I said.

"See you then. I'll have coffee waiting."

"You have enough to do without fetching me coffee."

"We have talked about this, Harper. You're much more pleasant when you're caffeinated."

I pouted. "I'm starting to feel like you're managing me."

"Somebody has to. See you in a bit."

I hung up and stood in my kitchen enjoying the last moments of silence. A long snore rolled from down the hall, reminding me that I wasn't alone. I padded back to my bedroom. The door was cracked and from inside, the sound of deep breathing came through.

The dark-skinned, muscled body I'd worshiped the evening before was sprawled across one half of my king-sized bed. The duvet had been tossed away like an afterthought at some point during the night. One arm was thrown over his face, a sheet tangled low enough around his waist that I could trace his Adonis lines to a well-groomed length if I so desired.

Jeremiah and I had been doing this for three months—meeting for a game or a movie or dinner, then stealing time with each other, no strings. He was a project manager at a tech company downtown. Funny, sexy, great in bed, and smart enough to let me control the speed and depth of our relationship. He did not ask questions I didn't want to answer. He texted or called, I responded if I felt like it.

And if I felt like it, I could wake up next to him taking up half of my bed.

I eased onto the edge of the bed and reached out, landing a hand on his shoulder, and rubbing his warm form. "Hey."

He stirred, squinting and groaning, twisting as he rolled toward me. I admired the wiry, sinewy muscles of his shoulders, his forearms, his back in the dim light. "Morning already?"

"Yep. And I've got to be in a bit early today. Just letting you know we're on a time clock this morning."

He grunted, then pushed out a heavy sigh. "So, no seconds then?"

I chuckled low, then slid a hand down the side of his body and below his taut belly, where I knew what was waiting for me, if I said the word. "Uh, that would be thirds, greedy. Rain check?"

"*Mmmmph.* Tore my ass up. You don't owe me shit." He stretched, looking around for his clothes. They were scattered across the floor where we'd left them. "What time is it?"

"Little after six thirty."

"Damn. I was knocked out." He sat up, scratching the stubble that had grown in overnight, sending an earthy sound into the air. "You got coffee on?"

"You know how I am about coffee. I've already had mine. You know where the to-go cups are."

"To-go cups." He mumbled, found his boxer briefs, pulled them on. "So, uh, you around next week? Maybe Thursday?"

"Honestly, I don't know yet."

I loosened the belt of my robe and let it slide from my shoulders. Typically, I slept in the nude and only wore a robe when I was not expected to be naked. I wasn't looking at him, but I knew he was eating up my full breasts, my hips, my ass, my thighs.

My feet.

This freak loved my feet.

"A new case is rolling in," I said, continuing like I didn't know he was slowly re-dressing while staring with his mouth open. "No telling how unpredictable work is about to get."

I heard the denim of his jeans rustle as he pulled them up his legs, then the zipper. He headed to the bathroom to use the spare toothbrush I kept handy for him.

"My boy that books TONIC night club said Maxwell was blowing through on some dinner and a show type shit," he called from the bathroom. "I can get you in if you wanna join. Let me know."

"I'll text you when I know if I'll be buried or not."

He grabbed his shirt and shoes and pulled them on, then made sure his wallet was in his back pocket. He leaned in only after taking one last long look at my naked breasts and kissed me.

"Enjoyed myself, as always," he said, before pulling back.

"As did I," I replied with a genuine smile. "I look forward to our next encounter."

"A'ight, I don't need the customer service voice. I'm going."

"Bye, fool. Lock my door on your way out."

I listened to him move through the apartment to gather his jacket and keys. The front door opened and closed and the deadbolt whirred after he entered the code to lock the door, leaving me to stand in the middle of the room looking at the rumpled sheets, the dent in the pillow where his head had been.

This was normal. It was what I insisted I wanted—physical intimacy without the risk of anything deep and meaningful and *dramatic*.

Men who were fine with texting when it was convenient and disappearing when it wasn't. Nothing formal. Just a good time.

Jeremiah was great for a good time, but he wasn't the type to drag to Sunday dinner with my family.

I stripped the bed, tossing the sheets and my robe into the hamper. Minutes later, I was in the shower, hot water and my favorite body wash sudsing away the night and his scent.

* * *

The drive to Ridgeway took thirty-eight minutes on average. I knew every light, every lane change, every moment when traffic would slow or open up. I had a playlist for the morning commute—Cardi B, Megan Thee Stallion, some Beyoncé when I needed to feel unstoppable.

By the time I pulled into my assigned spot in the employee garage, I'd already run through several songs and scenarios.

Best case: the Hart family was just looking for answers. We could provide them with transparency and compassion.

Worst case: the family was looking for someone to blame, and the hospital was already deciding who that someone would be.

Dr. Cole Vaughn's face flashed in my head like a blinking cursor.

I breezed through the employee entrance, taking the stairs to the fourth floor. The elevator was faster, but I liked the stairs. I got my steps in and it gave me time to shift from Harper-at-home to Harper-at-work.

Rowan was at their desk outside my office, short fade freshly lined, their usual uniform black button-down shirt and black slacks crisp against reddish brown skin. A silver wedding band caught the light as their fingers moved quickly across the low-profile keyboard.

They glanced up when I stepped out, already tracking me. A file folder was centered on the desk.

"Morning," they said, standing to hand me the file. "This is as complete as I can get it. An electronic copy is already in your inbox so you can bring it up on your iPad."

I took the folder and walked into my office, smiling over my shoulder when I noticed the mug of coffee waiting.

"You've got to stop spoiling me. Got me smiling in the morning and shit." I dropped my bag, then slid into my chair. "Anything pertinent since we talked earlier?"

"The patient's name was Earl Thomas Greene," Rowan read from the summary page. "Mr. Greene was a long-term resident at Brookside Assisted Living. The facility called 911 when they found him collapsed in his room. ER ran the protocol, did an ultrasound, found an aneurysm, and transferred to surgery. Next of kin is listed as Diane, his granddaughter. She's married to a Hart—"

"So he's not wealthy, but her granddaughter's husband is?"

"Correct."

"Brookside isn't where I'd put my grandfather," I mused. "Families don't take care of each other like they used to, do they? So Diane is saying we moved on her behalf without her consent? How long until she was informed of his death?"

"The facility says they called her when they found Mr. Greene in his room. She'd been out of town and was hard to reach. Then RMC notified her to call the ER when he was transferred to surgery, then again upon his passing, but it was four hours before anyone spoke with her."

"Four hours? She's throwing a fit and it took her four hours to call someone back?"

In a hospital, that could be a lifetime or an eye blink depending on the patient, the injury, the intervention. And whether someone was pushing for aggressive treatment or letting nature take its course.

I tabbed through the file. Mr. Greene had been seen at the ER quite a few times in the past few months. "His history sounds like he was at end of life. He was in his eighties. So she's saying what, exactly?"

"That nobody gave her a chance to be involved with his care, that her grandfather died alone because the hospital was in a hurry to cut somebody open."

"Now what kind of ridiculous bullsh—"

I paused, biting my tongue. My opinion had no place here. But I was frustrated because that narrative would drive everything from this point forward.

Hart family money meant the cause of Earl's death would be attributed to everything but him being an old man that died when his body gave out. They would dig deep, looking for medical error or malpractice or abandonment.

These kinds of claims made juries angry and hospital boards panic.

"What's the documentation look like?" I asked.

"It passed post mortem review."

"Hmm. Well, that's good." I scrolled through the file, flipping through the color-coded flags Rowan had already applied: yellow for missing information, orange for vague language. Red for timeline gaps that could raise questions.

"So, why is this case my problem?" I asked.

"Officially, because you're the best at what you do." Rowan stopped to smirk. "Unofficially? Probably because Diane Hart is Black and so is the surgeon."

My eyes rolled at that. I suppressed a heavy sigh. "When being a competent Black woman bites you in the ass," I said, reaching for the mug of coffee. "Let me read through this. I need you to rearrange my morning. Nothing new unless it's urgent. This is going to be a...well, you know."

"A shit show. Mmmhmmm. Already working on it." Rowan left quietly, pulling the door closed behind them.

I found Dr. Cole Vaughn's name in the notes. He'd assessed the patient, provided intervention. The intervention failed.

He'd done his job.

But had he done enough? That was the question Diane Hart and likely a very expensive lawyer was asking. That was the question I had to answer.

My phone buzzed. A text from my sister flashed on screen:

ALICIA:

Are you alive? You've been AWOL from the last two Sunday dinners. I miss your face.

I stared at the message, scrolling back in my mind. Had it been two weeks since I'd had dinner with my family? Probably.

Between work and the general exhaustion of being the only single person at a table full of couples and kids, Sunday dinners had become something I found reasons to avoid. Alicia would be with her partner. Aaron would bring his daughter. Even Naomi would show up with whoever she was dating this month and swearing she was about to marry. She was the most lovesick person I'd ever met.

I'd be the only one fielding questions from my mother about whether I was seeing anyone special and getting looks from my father that said he worried I worked too much.

I did not need their damn help to get a man. I had *plenty* of men.

ME:

My dry ass text message inbox says you ain't missed nobody's face. Lord willing and the creek don't rise, I'll be there this week.

ALICIA:

Good! And would it kill you to pretend to be dating someone? It would make the 'rents so happy in their golden years.

ME:

I will not be fake dating anyone to get a plate.

ALICIA:

Fine. See you Sunday. And I do be missing your face! Love you.

ME:

Love you too, Leesh.

I returned to the file and started building a plan to make sure the Hart family didn't sue the pants off of RMC. I was halfway through my second read when a Teams message popped up:

Rowan:

You in for Dr. Rice?

I frowned.

Me:

I don't suppose I can hide from her.

Dr. Rice walked in and closed the door behind her,

which meant this wasn't a casual check-in. "Morning, Harper. I see you're already digging into the Greene case."

"Morning, Liz. Yes, I'm reviewing the file now." I gestured to the chair across from my desk. "Coffee?"

"No, thank you. I'm already three cups in."

Dr. Elizabeth Rice settled into the chair with grace, crossing one long leg over the other. She was in her late fifties, polished and seasoned, graying hair in a sleek, shoulder length cut—more than a bob.

A *Robert,* if you will.

Liz wore expensive suits and even more expensive shoes and never drove; she used a car service.

"I missed the gala on Saturday. How was it?" I asked, keeping my tone light. "I saw the photos on the Foundation page."

"Exhausting but successful," she answered, as if she lifted a finger to do any work for it. "We raised over two million for the cardiac wing expansion." She adjusted a Cartier bracelet, ever so casually. "You should have come, Harper."

"You know how it is this time of year. I was buried alive." That, and I had no intention of paying for the privilege of spending my Saturday evening rubbing elbows with the blue blood crowd. "Did Natalie decide on a college, yet? It was between Stanford and..."

"She was between there and Wellesley, but Stanford won." Rice's smile warmed slightly. "We're thrilled, though the distance is going to take some getting used to."

I glanced pointedly at the file open on my desk, hoping to change the topic. I could only take so much of the part of office politics where I pretended to care about people's spouses and children.

"So, let's talk about the Hart case and why it's on my desk."

"Well, it's delicate," she said, after a pause. "Needs your steady hand."

"You're not kidding. We couldn't manage to keep the grandfather of one of our donors alive?"

"Diane and Eric Hart are not people we want upset, Harper. They have deep ties to this hospital. The Chairman of the Board knows them personally."

I kept my expression neutral. "And?"

"And," she continued after a moment, "the chairman has been in my inbox about this case already. We need to make sure this doesn't become an issue. I expect you to manage expectations all the way around."

I knew the drill: protect the institution and make sure the donor family doesn't decide to redirect their generosity elsewhere.

"OK. Well, like I said, I am reviewing the case."

"Of course." Dr. Rice paused. "And Harper—could you speak with Dr. Vaughn?"

"Why? Because he's Black?"

"Because if this inquiry escalates, we need to make sure the message is clear and unified."

I looked up, my brows raised and my hackles up. This case was already on my nerves. "The message?"

"That the hospital followed appropriate protocols. That any gaps in process were anomalies and not a breakdown they can pin on us."

There was the exit strategy. If someone had to take the fall, it wouldn't be Ridgeway Medical Center. It would be a single individual receiving a heavy dose of the blame.

"I'll review the case," I replied. "And I'll brief Dr. Vaughn."

Rice stood, her Colgate-white smile widening. "I know you will. That's why you're so good at this."

She left, closing the door behind her.

I pulled my laptop closer, then logged into email to send a message through the head of Trauma to arrange for a conversation with Dr. Vaughn.

Poor guy had no idea the system was already setting up to sacrifice him.

Chapter Two

COLE

I peeled off my scrubs and shuffled into the locker room; it was nearly six o'clock and I'd been on my feet all day, beginning at seven with rounds, then two surgeries, then a tense forty-minute conversation with a family who wanted to know why their father now needed a feeding tube when he was "fine" days ago.

Well, because he wasn't "fine". Because he'd had a stroke. Because his swallow reflex was affected, and if we didn't give him a tube, he'd choke or aspirate food and die of pneumonia.

But what actually came out of my mouth was softer, the way my mother had always taught me to speak when people were afraid, and not like I was offended that someone dared question my brilliance.

"You don't need to convince people that you're smart, son," she used to tell me. "Show them. They'll see it."

I changed into gym shorts and pulled a Xavier University t-shirt over my head, then headed down to the hospital's recreation center, which held a small gym and indoor courts for kickball, racquetball, or tennis. Tuesday night pick-up games had been a tradition since my first year at Ridgeway, trauma versus whoever showed up. Usually plastics or ortho, sometimes cardio if they were feeling brave.

The gym was tucked into the basement level of the building. The floor was scuffed, the hoops slightly crooked, but for a Tuesday night pick-up basketball game, it worked. I pushed through the double doors toward the familiar sound of rubber bouncing off hardwood.

"Vaughn!" someone shouted from the far end of the court. "'Bout time you brought your ass. We been waiting."

I walked over to where the usual suspects were warming up. Two from trauma—Dr. Banks, a surgeon I'd worked with that morning, and Dr. Kim. Joining them were three from plastics, including their behemoth of a fellow, Jackson, who had to be at least six foot six and two hundred and twenty pounds.

"Traffic was terrible," I said, grabbing the ball to silence the pounding against the floors. I shot at the hoop, just barely missing the net.

I wasn't warmed up yet.

"You work right upstairs," Banks pointed out, appearing confused.

"Still terrible."

We ran a quick game to fifteen. Trauma took it, with me sinking the final shot while Jackson tried and failed to block me.

"Man, how are you even making these?" he complained, bending over with his hands on his knees. "I'm literally almost a foot taller than you."

"All height, no skill," I joked, catching the ball Banks tossed back to me. The gym erupted in laughter and trash talk. We reset, then played another game.

This was my time, the only hour of the day when I wasn't Dr. Vaughn, trauma surgeon. I could just play.

Trauma won again, 15-13. Kim hit a three-pointer that had plastics calling foul even though everyone knew it was clean. We were about to line up for a third game when my phone rang. I glanced over at the bench, checking the name on the screen.

Dr. Marcus Webb, Surgery Chair. The high of our win evaporated, replaced by a cold knot in my gut.

"Shit, it's Webb. I'm probably getting my ass chewed about something. Give me a minute," I said, grabbing the phone and stepping into the hallway, letting the gym door swing shut behind me.

"Vaughn," I answered as I picked up.

"Evening, Dr. Vaughn. I hope you're well."

Webb's voice always carried a rich tenor, but sometimes it was warm the way a mug is warm right before you burn your hand. He could sound like your old college roommate or your favorite uncle right up until he told you your grant had been denied, or you were being audited, or whatever the bad news of the week was.

I'd learned not to take his tone as indicative of how the conversation might go, but there was no universe where a call from the Chair after hours meant anything good.

I wedged a shoulder against the cold cinder block, cradling the phone between cheek and collarbone as I watched the game through the small window in the door.

"I'm fine, Dr. Webb. What can I help you with?"

"Sorry to interrupt your evening. I need to give you a heads-up about a case coming through Risk regarding a patient death about six weeks ago, give or take. Elderly male, abdominal aneurysm. You were the surgeon on that one."

I remembered every death. He'd been bleeding out before he even made it to the OR. We'd tried everything, but there was nothing left to repair.

If Risk Management was looking into it, it meant someone had filed a complaint and the hospital was covering its bases before a lawsuit landed.

"I recall the case," I said, parsing my words carefully. "Nothing came up in post mortem review. What's the issue now?"

"Risk wants to do a standard review. You know how these things go. The family is grieving. They need someone to blame."

"That man was in his eighties, very frail and in ill health. Knowing he was dying when he was brought in, they're pointing fingers at me?"

"No one's pointing, Cole," Webb replied. "The family are donors to RMC, so we need to be completely sure that we were in process. To that end, you've got a meeting scheduled tomorrow morning with Harper Sutton, a director over in Risk. She will review the case, go over the timeline, ensure we're airtight. Standard procedure, straightforward process."

A review six weeks after the fact, even though the incident had cleared the post mortem—a session held after every patient death—was proof that this wasn't standard or straightforward.

"I guess," I said, instead of voicing my concerns. Even if

Webb knew the real story, he wouldn't share those thoughts with me.

"Thank you for taking the time. And Cole..." He paused, taking so long of a beat that I had to urge him to continue.

"Dr. Webb?"

"Keep your head clear and emotions in check. Be cooperative. Don't get defensive. This isn't personal; just dotting i's and crossing t's. We just need to answer the family's questions so this inquiry doesn't go any further."

"Don't make this worse by being myself, then."

Dr. Webb sighed. "If that's the way you need to frame it to come out unscathed—"

"Respectfully, Dr. Webb," I broke in, "I don't have anything to worry about. The treatment was warranted and appropriate and within policy."

"I don't doubt that. Just let them ask their questions, give your answers, and let it go. Don't turn this into something it doesn't need to be."

I wanted to ask what this could turn into, but it was better that I kept my mouth shut.

"Understood," I bit out.

"A calendar invite will follow shortly."

Webb hung up. I pressed the button to lock the phone, trying not to let my mind run away with itself. I couldn't help it, though.

If it were routine, Webb wouldn't have called me direct.

If this were just checking a box, Risk wouldn't be involved. I didn't need anyone to spell it out; I was the last name on the chart. Last hands to touch the patient.

Easy pickings.

I pushed back through the gym doors. A new game had

started, with plastics trying to capitalize on trauma being down a man. Banks saw me first and called a timeout.

"Everything good?" Banks called out, jogging over.

"Yeah. Fine." I grabbed my water bottle, took a long swallow. "Webb had to hit me up about something."

"OK. So, you coming back in or tapping out?"

I should go home. Review the Greene case. Pull up my notes, refresh my memory on every decision I'd made that day.

I glanced at the court, at Jackson setting up for an easy layup, at Kim already talking trash about how trauma couldn't win without their ringer.

"And pass up the chance to block Jackson all night? I'm in."

We played two more games. Trauma won both. By the time we called it, my shirt was soaked through and my legs felt like concrete, but my head was clearer than it had been all day.

We ambled toward the locker room, still talking trash. Banks elbowed me in the ribs as soon as we were out of earshot of everyone else.

"What's up with you? You didn't seem right when you came back in from that call."

I shrugged. "A death about six weeks back. I told you about it—old dude, aneurysm, bled out as soon as I got him open. A no-win situation from jump. Anyway, it's coming back up through Risk. I have a meeting with them in the morning."

"Oh, yeah?" Banks cocked an eyebrow, a sly expression crossing her face. "Who over there? I've got friends everywhere."

"Harper Sutton. You know her?"

Banks laughed. "Hell yeah, I know her," she replied, a smile lifting the corners of her mouth. "Fine as all hell. Smart. Doesn't take shit from anybody—admin, staff, family, whoever."

Her words confirmed what I knew of Harper. I'd sat in meetings with her. She had a smile that was disarming until you realized the questions she was asking were designed to trap you. She lived three steps ahead of everyone.

"She's pretty good," I said.

"Mmmhmmm," Banks hummed, putting a purr on it. "Good and *fine*."

I paused, then hit her with the slowest, coldest side-eye I could muster. "Why are you such a horndog tonight, Freida? Your girl out of town or something?"

She wrinkled her nose, her top lip curling. "Some conference, and then a girls' weekend in Miami. Can you tell I miss her?"

"Not at all," I said, laughing. "You couldn't go on the girls' trip? You're a girl."

"Nah, it's her girls from college and we've made it a point to not intermingle our friend groups. Her people are her people, mine are mine. But the second she hits that doorway?"

Banks grunted, bucking her hips in a shameless and lewd fashion.

"You are not doing any such thing," Kim cut in, sliding up behind us. "You respect the fuck outta Kris."

"You right. It'll just look like I don't for a couple minutes." Her gaze flicked to me, conspiratorial. "At least I get to live out my fantasies. Unlike Vaughn over here."

I shook my head, pushing through the men's locker room door. "You need help."

"Just saying what you're thinking," Banks called, ducking into the locker room.

The thing was...she had a point. Harper Sutton had my attention without trying to get it.

Deep skin tone, natural hair she wore out and full, or pulled back into a bun or a puff, big brown eyes, and a figure that she clothed in well-tailored designer suits. More than once I'd caught myself staring, then had to pretend I'd been deep in thought about something other than the shape of her ass cheeks as she walked past my chair.

Sometimes I'd catch myself wondering what she talked about when she wasn't discussing liability issues or hospital protocols. How different her laugh might be when she wasn't in professional mode. If those fashionable suits ever came off in favor of something more revealing.

I hated when I gave my mind over to idle fantasy, passing thoughts that were acknowledged then set aside because acting on them would be inadvisable for about a dozen reasons.

I showered quickly, the hot water beating against worn muscles, then changed back into street clothes before heading to the parking garage. As I slid behind the wheel of my Range Rover, my phone buzzed. The face that popped up on screen made me smile.

Talia, my youngest sibling, was technically my half-sister. My father died not long after I was born, leaving my mother, my two older brothers, and me. Mom met Walter Ellis when I was in junior high and fell hard. Soon after, she popped up pregnant with a baby she wasn't supposed to be able to have.

Even after I left for college and moved out of state, Talia and I stayed tight. We kept tabs on each other every few days and Tuesday evenings was her move because she knew I'd be shooting hoops after work and winding down on my drive home.

I swiped to answer the call, then started the engine so her voice would come through the car speakers. "What's up, kid?"

Talia scoffed. "Every damn week, I gotta remind you that I am an adult. You alive?"

"Barely," I replied, not even masking my fatigue. "Long day and I just got off the court."

"Who won?"

I frowned, centering my face in the screen. "You wanna ask me that shit again? I ain't no loser."

"My bad, damn. I was just making conversation."

"You need to come correct in your small talk. What's goin' on witcha?"

"Just heading home. And I know it's late. Shut up in advance."

I laughed, throwing the vehicle in reverse and pulling out of the space, then heading north toward my neighborhood. The city lights blurred past my window.

"What I look like yelling at you about leaving work late and I'm also leaving work late?"

"At least you had a fun excuse," Talia replied. "I had work, work, and more work."

"We celebrating your promotion yet?"

Talia also worked in healthcare, more on the patient support side, and had recently been pursuing a senior position.

"Nah, not yet. I'm still thinking about what you said when we talked last week," she said.

I flexed my hands on the steering wheel, recalling our conversation the week before. "What are you hung up on?"

She blew a stream of air through her teeth. "I'm the one implementing the cuts that I know are coming. I know they're looking at a reduction in patient navigation services —the people who actually help patients figure out their bills, their insurance, their options. I'm the one that's gonna take the heat."

I understood that tension, the gap between what made sense on paper and what actually would fly in real life. "I mean, yeah. But when that's all over, you have the chance to revamp your department. You can't fix the system from the outside, Tal."

"It doesn't sound like I would be fixing it from the inside either. I'd feel like I'm part of the problem, like they want someone to be the face of these changes they're making. I don't know if I want to be that face."

A car cut me off and I hit the brakes harder than necessary. "Then don't take it," I said, after talking myself out of flipping them off.

"Which leaves me in this role that feels like a dead end. I was hoping this promotion would be a way to move up."

I couldn't argue with her assessment and her desire for upward mobility. But I'd also played the game to get where I was and kept playing to stay here. I covered my ass like it was my full-time job and performed well enough that no one could question my competence.

In theory.

Traffic thinned as I left downtown behind. My neighborhood was fifteen minutes out, quiet streets and houses with yards. I rubbed the back of my neck with one hand.

"Look, take the job or don't, but whatever you decide, make sure it's because you chose it, not because you feel like it's your only way out. You're too good to let them make you feel like you gotta be the heavy. And don't sign on for that kind of weight on your shoulders without a whole lot of money. You feel me?"

She was quiet for a moment. When she spoke again, her voice was softer. "Felt. I'll think about it some more. They want to know my decision by Friday."

"Don't overthink it. It's right or it's not."

"Says the man who overthinks everything."

I grinned, tilting my head so I was in view of the camera. "That's different. Me overthinking stuff keeps people alive."

She laughed, and I could hear her relaxing. "Okay, trauma surgeon," she said, her tone moving into more teasing and less stressed. "What's up over that way?"

"Man...same shit, new day," I said.

My role in Talia's life was to be a sounding board, not to burden her. We'd talk about this case, my meeting with hospital administration and the threat to my reputation as a surgeon, but not until well after it had been resolved.

I pulled up to my house, a modest two-story home I'd bought when I was recruited to Ridgeway Medical. Three bedrooms, a small but nice yard on a quiet street. It was just enough for me, no matter how many of my friends and family tried to strong-arm me into renting them a room.

Ms. Patricia always left the porch light on when she came to clean. She was a no-nonsense Caribbean woman who called me either "Cole, dear" or "young man" depending on how much I'd irritated her that week.

Inside, the house smelled like a deep clean and the remnants of something savory. My mouth watered as I counted the hours since I'd had the Tuesday special in the cafeteria.

A note lay on the counter, written in Ms. Patricia's

careful cursive. I heard the curl of her tongue and the lilt in her voice as I read it:

> *I made stewed chicken with rice and vegetables. It's in the fridge. Just heat it up and enjoy. And Cole, dear, I need your items to add to the grocery list. I'll be shopping tomorrow and you're a picky boy.*
>
> *—ms p.*

In the fridge, I found the glass dishes. The chicken sat in a dark, seasoned sauce, the rice fluffy beside it, the vegetables cooked down and tender. The smell hit my nose first—thyme, garlic, something with heat. I liked to cook when I took the time, but Ms. Patricia cooked for me far better than I cooked for myself.

I heated up a plate in the microwave, grabbed a bottle of water, and carried both into my home office. The room was big enough for a desk, a bookshelf, and a leather desk chair. I sat down, pulled up the hospital system on my laptop, and logged in, going straight for my notes.

The file loaded slowly, page by page. I ate while I read, methodically working through the case. The intake notes from the ER. The ultrasound images. The decision to proceed under emergency protocol—it was all noted according to policies and procedures.

My surgical notes were clean, detailed. Every decision warranted, every rule followed.

I took a long pull from the bottled water and stared at the screen. What could the family be questioning, six weeks after Earl Greene's death?

And why didn't it feel like the hospital was backing me up?

I drew down the lid of my laptop and rubbed my thumbs across closed eyelids. The food had been good—Ms. Patricia's cooking always was—but my stomach felt heavy, weighed down by more than food.

I tried not to dwell on my meeting in the morning, but my mind kept looping back to Banks's offhand remark:

She's fine as all hell.

With a tired exhale, I stretched out, body slouched low in my chair, and relaxed my thighs until they fell open. I slid my hand over my abs and then lower, past the elastic of my sweats, to the insistent warmth beneath.

A long, slow breath left my lungs as I allowed myself a brief moment of disconnect from everything except the tingle of anticipation that had crept in and refused to leave.

I let the images come. Not the sterile flashes of Harper walking around the administration wing or through the halls of RMC, but the Harper Sutton I could only see in my fantasies.

I'd never seen her outside of work context, but I was good at filling in the blanks and details—like what her sexy, sultry voice sounded like when she wasn't being professional.

I let the fantasy spiral, let my carnal nature indulge in thoughts of what it would feel like to have all of her limbs wrapped tight around me, her body responding to mine. What she would sound like as her climax approached. How she would beg for more, harder, faster, deeper, not in the measured cadence of a work conversation but a ragged cry torn from her throat as she clung to my shoulders, the better to grind and rut her warm center against me.

I'd been working myself in a slow, methodical rhythm,

but as the images took hold, my grip tightened and my pace quickened until I was chasing release with desperate urgency.

My wrist flicked and tightened as I sped up. Flames spiraled up from my groin. My breaths were harsh, my hips thrusting, not even pretending to be anything but an animal in that moment.

The vision of her, head thrown back, eyes narrowed in lust, mouth open, hips rolling against me, was so vivid that I was panting her name audibly, the sound ricocheting off the walls and hard surfaces of my office.

Harper...yeah... fuck...that's it...ride it...ride me hard baby...Harper...sssshitttt...Harper...Harper...I— fuck, I'm comin'...Harperr—

I arched in the chair, jaw clenched, thighs quivering as I pumped at a frantic, frenzied pace. I let go only when I couldn't hold back anymore, shuddering as I soaked the inside of my sweats, plastering sticky heat over my fist.

The force of the climax left me momentarily stunned, my pulse a dull roar in my ears. For a moment, I sat with my head angled back against the leather chair, my eyes shut and my palm gripping my dick like I'd been choking it. Aftershocks rippled through my body until every muscle gradually unclenched.

The fantasy still hovered at the edges of my mind, Harper's name ricocheting like a burned-in afterimage.

Did I really just jack off to a daydream about a woman who might be directing my career implosion?

Yeah. And it was honestly the release I needed.

I stood, snatching a handful of tissues from the box on my desk, and mopped up as best I could, then headed upstairs. A half-hour later, I rolled into bed, set my alarm, then settled in, listening to the silence of the house.

I told myself I liked it this way, that I craved peace and being able to hear myself think.

But...

What if I could roll into bed behind a tall, leggy, thick, sexy woman who had just ridden the fuck out of me and was ready for more?

Chapter Three

HARPER

I arrived at the conference room early just to get set up. There was an art to an effective meeting.

The chairs needed to be positioned just so—close enough to encourage collaboration, but not so close that anyone felt crowded. I moved the head chair slightly away from the table, creating a subtle power dynamic that would work in my favor. The lighting dimmed with a touch of the control panel, the morning sun casting the room in a glow that made people more agreeable.

I pulled out a chair for Dr. Vaughn and set it across from me. I wanted to be able to catch his expression when he answered my questions, but there had to be a little space between us.

Laptop open, file cued up, the key sections flagged so I

could find them without looking unprepared. Legal pad on my left, pen next to it, iPad off to the side.

I'd dressed with intent. Dark suit tailored but not tight because there's a difference between a good fit and trying to seduce someone. Cream silk blouse, soft against my skin and adding a touch of elegance. Hair slicked back, not a strand out of place. Small gold hoops, discreet but catching the morning light.

The conference room door swung open and Dr. Vaughn strolled in, pausing just inside the threshold, the heavy wood door closing quietly behind him. He took in the room, cataloging the experience—the generic hospital style artwork on the walls, the mid-size table with its arrangement of water glasses and pens in the center, the monitor at the head of the room blinking in standby mode.

He wore dark slacks and a polo shirt open at the collar, showing off lean muscle and slightly hairy forearms. A leather messenger bag was slung casually over one shoulder.

Every line of him said he did not want to be in this room.

"Dr. Vaughn." I stood, hand out. "Thank you for making time this morning."

His handshake was quick, all business, zero warmth. "Ms. Sutton."

"Harper is fine," I said, motioning to the empty chair. "Go ahead and have a seat."

He dropped the bag to a chair but didn't sit. Instead his eyes fell to my laptop, the Greene file, then bounced back to my face.

"Before we start, let's talk about what this meeting is actually about."

I sat, my hands folded on the table. "This meeting is for us to understand your perspective on Mr. Greene's death so we can address the family's concerns with all of the knowledge needed."

"That's the official answer," he said, still standing. "What's the real one?"

I met his stare. Dark, guarded, wary. He likely thought I was here to build a case against him and I couldn't blame him. That's what someone in my seat would do if they were looking to pin a death on someone.

I decided to do the unexpected. I dropped the bright, earnest cadence I used with families and relaxed, leaning my arms on the table.

"All right, I'll be straight with you," I said. "The real answer is that the Hart family has retained counsel. They're looking for any opening on the Greene case—clinical error, negligence, failure to document, even something as minor as a missed phone call. Their attorney is aggressive, and they've already started sending requests for records. If they find something actionable, we're looking at depositions and a formal complaint to the medical board. My job is to get ahead of them and shut it down before anybody gets burned."

Pausing, I watched him process the directness, the lack of euphemism, the acknowledgment of the legal minefield beneath his work.

"Anybody?" He pulled out the chair and sat, directing his body toward me. "That's an interesting word to use, considering I'm the only person that actually worked on him that got called into a meeting."

"Would you rather I said *you*?"

"I'd rather you be real with me. I didn't act alone, but none of us should be under scrutiny. Our conduct was not against policy."

"You're right." I laced my fingers together, conceding

that Cole had made excellent points. "Diane Hart thinks she should have been consulted before a single cut was made on her grandfather. Admin is nervous because the Harts are donors and friends with the chairman. And you're the surgeon on the chart, the person who performed the procedure. This puts a target on your back."

Cole's jaw tensed, a muscle flexing along his cheek. "So you're here to let me know that RMC is going to pin this death on me."

"No, Dr. Vaughn. I'm here to *keep* the family and administration from pinning this death on you."

He stared at me for a full beat, and in that time, I watched a slow-motion calculation happen behind his eyes. A recalibration of sorts, trying to figure out if I was really on his side.

I didn't break eye contact. I let the silence drag out, my posture unchanged, hands loose, not even pretending to make notes or glance at the laptop.

Eventually, Dr. Vaughn relaxed his jaw, enough that the set line of his mouth softened and his shoulders visibly dropped. I hid my satisfaction at his reaction.

I hadn't won him over yet.

"So, the Hart family complaint centers on notification and consent. Walk me through your decision to move ahead with surgery."

He exhaled, shaking his head. "By the time we got him on the table, he was bleeding out. Policy says we don't have to wait for consent. I didn't."

"The specific note is that the family wasn't adequately informed of the severity of his condition."

Cole's eyebrows shot up. "As I came to understand it, the family wasn't *reachable* to be informed. Maybe they should be talking to intake."

I flipped a page in my notes. "The family's attorney will argue that you prioritized performing a complicated surgery over proper communication—because they *would have* told you to wait. They allege the hospital failed to keep the family informed at critical junctures."

"Was I supposed to let him bleed to death while I waited for someone to pick up the phone?"

"I'm not saying you should have done anything differently, Dr. Vaughn. I'm getting the lay of the land and the case from your perspective. And I'm telling you what the family's attorney is going to argue."

"Which is *what*? The family thinks I'm a showboat looking for any opportunity to cut? He died on my operating table in a room full of people while I was trying to clamp his aorta," Cole argued, his jaw clenched so tight the words sounded snapped off. "There was no one to 'be with him' because I was up to my elbows in his blood."

Anger flared like a pulse thrumming under the skin. He would never believe me, but I understood his position. Cole was a mere mortal who was supposed to be a god. Instead, he'd watched someone die under his watch and had to justify why he couldn't perform miracles.

I softened my stance and my tone. "I'm not here to judge your clinical decisions. From what I can see in the chart and our discussion today, you did everything by the book—"

He cut me off. "I'm waiting for the *but*."

"*But*...perception is what matters here. When the attorney starts picking apart our timeline, they'll only care about whether we followed protocol. Whether Mr. Greene's family was contacted at every juncture, and whether he received an appropriate standard of care."

"Appropriate standard of care," he repeated in a brittle

tone. "That man received world-class care in a renowned hospital by a skilled surgeon. He was going to die no matter what I did."

I nodded once. "I understand."

"So," he said, angling back with his arms spread wide across the chairs next to him. "Is this the part where you work your magic, make the hospital shine, and I get the shit end of the stick?"

As if he realized he'd let loose, he sat up straight. "I—pardon me. Excuse my language."

"You're fine, Dr. Vaughn." I smiled, assuring him I wasn't offended. "If I wanted to position your role as expendable, I'd be taking a different approach entirely."

His eyes narrowed, calculating. "Do tell."

"I'd zero in on the rush to surgery, of course. I'd paint a picture of a cowboy with a scalpel instead of the surgeon who's never had a complaint here at RMC."

I paused for effect, letting him know I'd researched him thoroughly. "I'd be laying out a case that paints you as reckless, not the competent, skilled surgeon I find you to be."

Cole studied me, the lines of his face shifting. Not trust yet. But something close flickered behind his eyes. "Why *aren't* you asking those questions?"

"Because Stevie Wonder can see that Mr. Greene's death was imminent, no matter what anyone did and when anyone was notified. Nothing short of divine intervention would have saved him."

I leaned in, lowering my voice. "And between us? When the hospital needs someone to blame, they never pick themselves. Who do you think is next in line?"

The silence in the room thickened, crowded in with the understanding of what remained unsaid.

"So, what's your angle?" he finally asked. "You work for the hospital."

"And so do you. I mitigate risk for RMC, but I'm also here to make sure every clinician with patient exposure follows policy. And when I'm satisfied that they have, I stand on that. I won't let anyone question their integrity. Mr. Greene's outcome was tragic, but his treatment here at RMC was appropriate. I will defend that position vigorously."

Dr. Vaughn's eyes lingered on mine for a long moment. He seemed to still be sizing me up, but eventually, he gave a slow nod. "Alright. What do you need from me?"

My coffee was cold by the time we finished our review, but my legal pad was full of notes. The air between us had changed, the earlier hostility dissolving into something closer to collaboration.

Cole glanced at his watch, his mouth dropping open. "Not to be rude, but I need to get down to ICU. Are we good?"

I hadn't realized how much time had passed. "For now, yes. Thank you for your time." I closed my laptop and stacked my notepad and iPad. "If I have questions, I'd like to reach out to you directly. Not through Dr. Webb."

He pulled out his phone, swiped to contacts, and handed it across the table. "Put your number in. I'll text you so you've got mine."

I keyed in my personal number, already feeling like some of our discussions would not be welcome on the official record. Then I saved it and slid the phone back to him.

"Thank you for being straight with me," he said, getting to his feet. "I appreciate being treated like a professional. Most administrators try to manage me."

"Well..." I smiled and started gathering the papers, the

folders, the pens I'd scattered across the table like breadcrumbs. "I try hard not to be most people in administration."

"I feel that." The undercurrent in his tone made me look up. "Keep that up." He swung his bag onto his shoulder and left.

A few minutes later, I followed, noting three problems I hadn't had when I walked in:

First, Cole Vaughn was going to be impossible to protect because he was too angry to play the game Risk Management wanted him to play.

Next, RMC wouldn't hesitate to sacrifice him if that's what it came to, and I was going to have to decide how far I'd go to stop them.

Last...I was already looking forward to seeing Dr. Vaughn again.

When I returned to the office suite, Rowan was hunched at their desk, glasses sliding down their nose.

"How'd it go?"

I crossed to my office, depositing my laptop and files on my desk, and collapsed into my chair. "About as well as you can imagine it would go if you accused a well-regarded surgeon of fucking up."

Rowan took up their usual place in the door frame, arms folded, lips bent in a half-smile. "So he won't just crawl under the bus for RMC? Damn."

I flipped open my laptop, the file and my notes waiting for me. "Nope."

"At least he's smart. Some of these MDs..." They clicked their tongue and shook their head at the thought.

"Which is almost worse," I said, glancing up at them. "He knows the hospital is setting him up and he's not about to play along with that narrative."

I averted my eyes before I added, "And I don't blame him."

"Oh, Lord," they replied, laughing a little. "You *like* Dr. Vaughn."

I didn't look up again. "I respect his position. I'm a woman with a job to do."

"Mmmhmmm."

I laughed, albeit nervously. "Don't start, Rowan."

"*You* don't start." The grin was impossible to ignore. They eased themselves away from the doorway, strolling over to my desk, leaning on the edge. "You know how you get."

"Wait, how do I get?" I arched a brow, already knowing this script too well.

"You are about to go to war over this man."

I closed my laptop, pushing out an exasperated sigh "I'm supposed to let them sacrifice a good surgeon because rich people need a scapegoat?"

"You're supposed to do exactly what you're doing. Just be careful. This case has money and politics all over it, and that means it won't be fair. If you get too close to the blast radius—"

"I know, Rowan."

"I know you know, Harper. And yet, you see someone getting railroaded and you become their personal defender."

I wanted to argue. I couldn't. "I hear you. I'll be careful."

After they left, I went back through the facts, stacking them up in my head. The more I worked, the clearer it became—the Hart family wanted someone to pay for the death of their loved one. The hospital wanted to protect itself. Those two wants didn't fit together unless someone took the fall.

My phone vibrated against the polished wood of my desk. I snatched it up, flipping it over to check the screen.

UNKNOWN NUMBER:

This is Cole Vaughn. You have my number now.

I stifled a smile, then saved his contact info and fired off a reply, thumbs quick on the glass.

ME:

Confirmed. I'll reach out once I've met with the family, their attorney, and Dr. Rice.

Three dots appeared immediately. Disappeared. Appeared again.

COLE:

Appreciate the heads up. Let me know if you need anything else from my end.

ME:

Sure will. A word of advice: don't answer any questions without a representative. If they're trying to build a narrative, don't give them ammunition.

His response came faster this time.

COLE:

Noted.

I set my phone down, but the screen lit up again before I could look away.

COLE:

I believe you meant what you said. About protecting me, not just the hospital.

My fingers hovered above the keys, stilled in midair. This was the moment I could and should draw a thick, bright line to keep a professional distance with Dr. Vaughn. To remind him—okay, myself—I had a job to do and I couldn't let anything personal bleed into it.

But I didn't do that.

ME:

I did mean it. Don't trust me too much yet though, Dr. Vaughn. I still work for RMC, even if I don't always agree with how they operate.

COLE:

Fair enough.

COLE:

AND IT'S COLE. I ONLY MAKE PEOPLE CALL ME DR. VAUGHN IF I DON'T LIKE THEM.

This time, I didn't fight a smile.

ME:

Fine, Cole. Then it's Harper.

COLE:

Already was.

A laugh slipped out, louder than I'd intended, echoing across the empty office. My fingers were already tapping out a reply.

ME:

See, every MD is a little bit of an asshole. Might rethink my approach.

COLE:

No take-backs. You're in too deep.

I was still smiling when I set the phone face-down on my desk and forced myself back to work.

By four o'clock, my eyes were tired and my coffee was cold again, but I'd built a preliminary strategy to protect Ridgeway Medical Center—and its staff—in our meeting with the Hart family. It wasn't perfect, but it was a start.

My phone rang. A glance at the screen made me groan aloud. I let it go for two rings before picking up.

"Hello, Liz. You're working late tonight."

"Harper, hi. Catch me up on your meeting with Dr. Vaughn."

I leaned back in my chair, already anticipating where this was headed. "It was positive overall. Productive. He's reasonable, and I don't see any red flags from a liability perspective."

I heard her soft exhale on the other end of the line. "That's reassuring." Papers shuffled, followed by the click of her office door. "And his attitude during the meeting? Did he seem receptive to the plan?"

The subtext was clear. She wanted to know if he'd roll over when the time came.

"He's frustrated, to be honest," I said, choosing my words carefully. "Which is understandable. But he's willing to work with us to address the family's concerns."

"That's what I wanted to hear." Another pause, long and tense. I picked up my pen, tapping it against my desk, waiting her out. "Harper, you do realize the stakes here, how delicate this situation is, right? The Hart family has considerable influence, and if they decide to make this death an issue—"

"I understand, Liz."

"Be sure you do. I need to know you're approaching this

the right way. Dr. Vaughn is an excellent surgeon, but surgeons don't always see the bigger picture."

The pen stilled in my hand. "You brought this to me, Liz. Dumped it right in my lap. Either you believe I can handle it properly or you don't."

"I wouldn't have brought it to you otherwise, Harper," she said, her tone cool as ice over the line. "I simply want to know if Vaughn is going to be a problem."

"Only if you disagree that Dr. Vaughn is competent and his management of this case was above board. If we position this as his failure, we're setting ourselves up for a situation that will hurt more than if the Hart family withdraws their support."

"It's not my goal to imply that Dr. Vaughn is incompetent."

"Then what is the goal?"

"I just need you to manage the situation, to make sure that when that attorney starts asking questions, we have clear answers that protect RMC. We don't need to give them any soft spots to target."

"I can do that." I kept my voice level even as my jaw tightened. "But I won't do it by helping RMC sacrifice a good surgeon."

"No one is asking you to." But her tone said otherwise. "Keep me updated. And Harper? Remember whose side you're on."

She hung up before I could respond. My jaw clenched so tight my teeth ached.

Remember whose side I was on?

I was on the hospital's side—and that included Dr. Vaughn.

The sun was starting to sink below the hills, casting long shadows across the parking lot. Somewhere in the building,

Cole was finishing his day, talking to families, doing the work that had gotten him into this mess in the first place.

And somewhere in Administration, people were deciding how to protect themselves at his expense.

I slid behind the wheel of my car and turned Megan Thee Stallion up until the speakers vibrated, letting heavy bass lines drown out my thoughts for the slow crawl through rush hour traffic. Forty minutes later, I pulled through the gates of my apartment complex, the sky a beautiful gradient of orange and pink.

Inside, I kicked off my heels, let my bag drop to the couch, and padded barefoot into the kitchen. I pulled a bottle of Malbec from the wine fridge and poured a glass, then carried it to the living room, settled onto the couch, and sat in the dark.

The day replayed in my mind like a film I couldn't stop watching.

The betrayal in Cole's eyes when I told him the hospital would always protect itself first.

The slight tremor in his voice when he talked about losing Mr. Greene.

The strong, capable surgeon's hands with veins roped along the back that curled into fists while he fought to keep his composure.

The burnt umber hue of his skin.

The silk of his deep tenor and how it wrapped around each word.

The distinguished silver threads weaving through the hair at his temples, tracing a path down to frame his jawline.

The shoulders that strained against his shirt, a hint of rippling muscle as he moved.

The truth hit me like a slap: I *wanted* Cole Vaughn. Not his medical expertise or professional guidance. I wanted his hands on me, his tongue dueling with mine, his body pressed to every inch of me.

I carried my wine to the bedroom, where city lights filtered through the curtains in thin stripes. After setting the glass on my nightstand, I shed my suit jacket, then the pencil skirt, followed by the blouse, lace bra, and finally my panties.

The overhead fan sent cool currents across my bare skin, raising goosebumps.

From my bedside drawer, I retrieved my favorite toy, my most reliable companion for nights when my mind needed emptying and I needed to get off without having to call Jeremiah. I didn't want his voice or his hands or his...*anything* crowding out what I actually wanted to picture.

I settled into the familiar hollow of my mattress, parting my thighs. With my eyes shut against the darkness, I switched on the rose vibrator and pressed its silicone petals against my clit.

The low hum filled the quiet room as I let my mind drift back to earlier in the day when it was just him and me and a closed door.

My breathing deepened as the vibrations sent waves through me. In my fantasy, it wasn't the rose toy against my skin. It was Cole's mouth, his stubble rough on my inner thighs. I imagined his dark eyes locked on mine as he licked and sucked, my fingers twisting the sheets as waves of heat pulsed through my core.

The fantasy shifted. Now it was his hands gripping my hips, positioning me exactly where he wanted me. Those surgeon's hands that had tried to save lives today now focused entirely on driving me wild. I pressed the toy harder, my free hand sliding up to cup my breast, fingers rolling my nipple as I pictured Cole's mouth replacing my touch.

"Unnnhhh...yes," I breathed, words dissolving into a whimper. "Cole, *please*."

I turned the toy up, adding pressure. My body responded instantly, hips rolling, heat and lightning twisting low in my belly. I imagined him whispering filthy things against my skin, his mouth everywhere, kissing my face, my neck, my breasts, sucking my nipples into taut buds like he couldn't get enough.

"What do you want?" I heard in my mind, his tone husky, rough, possessive.

"I want you to fuck me," I whispered aloud. "Fuck me hard. Fuck me deep. Fuck me slow."

The fluttering, sucking pulse of the rose sent a full-body shudder coursing up my spine, so intense I had to bite my lip to keep my neighbors from hearing me scream as I mentally begged for his hands, his mouth, his body pinning me between him and the firmest of mattresses. I arched high, imagining my nails digging into his skin, making him smile and nudge my knees wider, my legs higher, then bury himself inside me with a steady, relentless rhythm.

I matched the imagined cadence of his thrusts, panting his name into the darkness, desperate for the release I could feel coiling inside me like a spring.

"Oh, God! Fuck...oh! God! Yes! Yes! Yes!"

The words tumbled out, rough and wild, my head thrown back as I lost control. The syllables hit the ceiling and rained down on me with every pulse. Suddenly I was neither in the room nor in my own skin but unraveling from the inside out.

The rose was relentless against my clit, but it was thinking about him, his chest pressed to mine, hips pounding our bodies together, rolling his pelvic bone against my clit that dragged the climax out, made me gasp his name again and again.

Fantasy layered over reality, blurring the line until I didn't know which was silicone-inspired and which was my own fevered imagination.

As the high faded, smaller waves rolled and I sought them out in greedy fashion. My hips jerked against the toy, whimpers caught behind clenched teeth, leaving nothing behind.

When I was boneless and wrecked, watching the ceiling fan rotate, I managed to switch the toy off and drop it beside me with a shaky hand.

Whew.

This was bad.

I mean, it was so good, so *fucking* good.

But bad that all I wanted was to be with that man for real. The ache of that wanting burned hotter than anything else.

The last of my wine was gone in two hard swallows. The fantasy kept looping—his hands, his body, his mouth sucking the ever-loving shit out of my pussy lips.

I set the empty glass down, dragged my body up, and headed to the shower, telling myself that despite the lingering aftershocks and mental images, I wasn't going for round two.

But then I turned around and grabbed the rose anyway.

Just in case.

Chapter Four

COLE

Something was off about the surgical bay.

It was cavernous and eerily quiet where monitors should beep and techs should murmur. I hovered over the draped form on the table, my hands moving through prep motions for a procedure I had no memory of scheduling and wasn't even sure what I was here to do.

My fingers groped for a scalpel. The instrument tray was empty. I yanked open a drawer, found it bare. Then another. When I touched the patient, my latex gloves came away slick and crimson red.

What the...

"I need some help in here," I called, turning toward the door.

Harper Sutton stood just in the doorway, arms folded

tight across her chest. Not moving, not speaking. Just watching me fail.

My eyes flew open into darkness and my bedroom came into focus. I inhaled deeply, exhaling slowly to calm my racing nerves as the nightmare dissolved.

I reached for my phone on the nightstand: 4 AM. I tossed back the covers, swung my feet to the floor, and shuffled to the bathroom where I pulled on gym clothes, brushed my teeth, ran a comb through my hair.

Then I headed downstairs, grabbing my keys and wallet from the kitchen counter before stepping outside.

The ten-minute drive to the gym wound through empty streets still slick with overnight rain. My headlights tracked a small animal skulking between parked cars; beyond that, only distant taillights.

I left the radio off. I didn't need the noise.

This gym wasn't anything special, a twenty-four-hour chain that lured people in with pizza and upsold them on memberships. Not saying I fell for the gimmick, but I did appreciate the post-workout slice every so often.

At this hour, the space held just three patrons: a woman pounding away on a treadmill with her headphones on, and two men hovering over free weights like long-time residents. No one made eye contact. That was the whole point of getting to the gym early.

I claimed my favorite rowing machine, still smelling faintly of bleach cleaner. I set the resistance and began pulling. The first few strokes were rough—my shoulders stiff from yesterday's surgeries and a game of pick-up basketball. Soon, the motion fell into a steady cadence: pull, breathe, release, breathe. The cables resisted each stroke and I leaned into it. By minute fifteen, sweat traced down my temples, and my shoulders were on fire.

This was the only part of my day that made sense. Effort in, result out.

After thirty minutes, I moved to the leg machines. My muscles screamed with every rep but my brain finally shut up. When I finished, my legs were shaking and the burn in my calves was welcome.

I did a half-hearted stretch, spent a few minutes letting the heat seep into my muscles in the sauna, and then headed home. I cracked the windows as I drove, the frigid air drying the sweat on my body, making the rest of me feel wired and alive.

A few minutes later, I was standing in the kitchen, staring at the counter and weighing my options: eggs or a protein shake. The shake would be easier. More protein too.

I grabbed the blender and tossed in frozen berries, a banana, pineapple, and a scoop of powder that claimed it tasted like vanilla, though it never really passed for the real thing.

I heard a key turning in the lock and the security system beeping. Ms. Patricia's footsteps sounded through the living room, heading straight for me.

"Cole Terrence Vaughn."

My whole government name. I didn't turn but did greet her as always. "Morning, Ms. Patricia."

She moved through my kitchen like she owned it. At sixty-two years old, she was spry and lively with caramel-toned skin, hair always pulled tight in a headwrap. Today it was a burnt orange, deep and rich, matching her scrubs and those battered Crocs she wore during her overnight nursing home shifts.

She zeroed in on the blender. "Tell me you are not about to have that mess for breakfast."

I shrugged, my thumb pressing the button. The blender

roared loud enough to cover anything else she might have said. When it cut out, I poured the shake into a glass and stuck a straw in.

"Just had a workout. I need the protein."

She shook her head. "That doesn't stick to the ribs and give you energy. Stew chicken is also protein. I left you plenty last night."

"Mmhmm. It was good."

"Was. You ate it *all*?"

"I didn't know I was supposed to portion it out. I was hungry."

She tugged the refrigerator open, peered inside, then clicked her tongue, already disappointed in whatever she saw. "Did you make that grocery list I asked for?"

She already knew the answer. I took a long sip of my shake and tried not to grimace. Thank goodness I'd tossed in some fruit; otherwise, it would have been straight-up chalk.

"Cole..."

"I'll do it," I said before she could get rolling.

She folded her arms and glared. "I'm going to the market today, and if you don't tell me what you want, you're getting what I think you need."

"That's fine." I set the glass down.

"No, it's not *fine*," she shot back, planting her fist on her hip. "Because you'll complain that I bought the wrong kind of chicken, or the ground beef isn't lean enough, or the bread isn't the kind you like—even though you never tell me which kind you like."

She pointed straight at a chair and demanded, "Sit. I'm making you breakfast, and you're making that list before you leave."

"I have to be at the hospital by seven," I tried.

She raised her eyebrows. "Then you had better get to it, hadn't you?"

Ms. Patricia had spent years running a household with four kids, six grandkids, and a schedule that would break most people. For the past few years, she'd been coming to clean, do laundry, and make sure I didn't forget to eat. She was old enough to be my aunt, if not my mother, and she did not play.

I sat.

She cracked eggs into a bowl one-handed, whisked them with hot sauce and black pepper, and poured the mixture into a buttery pan.

I opened my phone and checked the day. Rounds with interns, ICU coverage, then the weekly department meeting. The evening was wide open, which meant paperwork.

"You're frowning at that phone like it hurt your feelings."

I looked up as she slid a plate in front of me with eggs, fluffy and golden, and toast just the right side of crisp. It smelled like actual food, not the shake I'd been choking down.

"Work," I said.

She placed a glass of orange juice in front of me. "You need a little sugar and some citric acid. Eat. And write that list."

A notepad and pen appeared, sliding toward my elbow.

I picked up the pen, tried to think. "Eggs. Bread. Chicken. Ground beef..."

She stopped me with a look. "Don't be an asshole, young man. What cut of chicken? Breast? Thigh?"

"The kind you usually get."

She was relentless. "Boneless? Bone-in?"

"Whatever's on sale, Ms. P. You're the one cooking it."

She made a little disgusted noise that said I was beyond help. "You're the one eating it, Cole! Be specific or I'm buying you turkey bacon and almond milk."

That was a threat. I hated both.

With a sigh, I started over and made the list detailed enough to pass inspection. The eggs were legitimately good —I hadn't realized how hungry I was until I started eating.

Ms. Patricia perched at the kitchen island with her coffee, watching me over the rim. "Cole, dear. You seem stressed. Tell Ms. Patricia what's goin' on."

"I'm fine, Ms. P."

"So, we lie now?" She gave me the side-eye and her classic head tilt. "You've been grumpy and quiet for days. I'm not just the housekeeper. I notice things."

I cleaned my plate and didn't bother answering because Ms. Patricia could spot a lie from the driveway.

"Is it a woman?"

My heart lurched. "It's never a woman."

"Mmmmm..." She tilted her head, giving me the look she reserved for when she knew I was hiding something. "You've got a look that calls you a liar."

"I do not have a look," I said a little too quickly. After a beat, asked, "What look?"

"Men get a kind of look when they're thinking about someone special." She smiled, took a sip, watched me. "Though sometimes that look means they're about to do something I wouldn't approve of."

"Well, I am a man, so..." I stood to take my empty plate to the sink. "I need to get ready. Full day."

"Will you have dinner at home tonight?"

"Don't know. Depends on how the day goes, but you know me—whatever you leave, I'll eat."

She picked up the notepad and checked my list. "Much

better. Not great, but better." She folded it and dropped it in her purse. "Cole?"

She waited until I turned to face her.

"Whatever's bothering you at that hospital—don't let them make you question yourself. You worked hard to get here. Fight to stay here."

I didn't have a good reply. I gave her a nod and headed out, grateful for the advice even if I wasn't sure how to use it.

The morning rhythm was already in full swing when I stepped through the doors at RMC. Residents clustered by the coffee station, hands wrapped around paper cups, someone's pager shrieking down the corridor and a low-grade chaos that buzzed beneath it all. I offered a few nods but didn't slow down.

My office was utilitarian, nothing more. Desk, chair, computer, a set of medical texts filling a shelf for appearances' sake. I hadn't cracked them open in years—not since every answer I needed was a click away. No photos, no mementos. Just a spot to read charts, type notes, and occasionally dodge an administrator if the day called for it.

My phone vibrated in my pocket. A quick glance told me I had a text.

DR. WEBB:

My office when you get in.

I stared at the message. Webb was seasoned and levelheaded. We'd worked side by side for years with never a problem, but if he wanted to see me face-to-face, it wasn't a social call.

I stood and headed upstairs.

Webb's office was a few floors above mine, housed among the frosted-glass doors that dotted the administrative suites. Corner spot, naturally. Windows from floor to ceiling, sunlight pouring in and bouncing off his desk—a slab of mahogany so polished you could check your tie in it. Leather guest chairs, diplomas on the wall in expensive frames. A family photo was strategically placed on the credenza: Webb, his wife, and two college-aged kids, all beaming on some sandy beach.

I knocked, stepping inside when he called my name.

"Cole. Have a seat."

He motioned to the chair across from him. Webb was in shape, the kind of lean that came from swimming laps and riding the Peloton before most people hit snooze. He still had a full head of hair but wore reading glasses on a chain around his neck. He'd gone from the OR to admin without anyone calling him soft. People still listened to and respected him.

"Morning, Dr. Webb," I said, taking a seat.

"Morning. Sorry for the abrupt summons. How'd your meeting with Ms. Sutton go?"

I shrugged. "Fine. It was the first pass. We went through the paperwork, combed the notes, talked about what the family might say if they decide to push the issue."

"Do they have a case?"

I shook my head. "I don't see it. Ms. Sutton didn't look convinced, either."

He grinned, but it didn't stick. "Well, we pay her well to be skeptical."

Webb leaned back, crossed one leg over the other. "Risk and Legal are meeting with the Hart family soon. If it goes beyond the initial review, you'll know."

"Goes beyond how?"

"Litigation. Right now it's just noise. A lot of questions, some complaints. A bit of a temper tantrum, honestly."

"Am I being named in an action or something?"

"No," he answered, too quickly to make me feel better. "You're part of the care team. You're the face, yes. But that's it."

I ran the scenario in my head. Part of the care team. Not responsible, but close enough to catch the heat if it came.

"What do you need from me?"

"Nothing yet. Just be available if they circle back with more questions." His tone grew lower, quieter, heavier. "Dr. Vaughn, be careful. You know, how you talk about the case. Be careful who you talk to about this case, inside or outside the hospital."

"Be careful? Meaning?"

"Meaning..." he said, drawing out the word as if I should know what he meant. "The family has retained counsel. Anything you say to anyone, even as a joke, could end up in a deposition. They can use anything. I need you on your best behavior."

When I left his office, I was more tense than when I'd gone in.

Be careful, don't say anything to anyone meant there was a live wire somewhere.

Don't worry meant I should pretend not to notice the live wire.

I was behind, so I cut through the admin to the ICU. I needed to clear my head and focus on the job.

* * *

The ICU was a zoo, with several patients recovering from a multi-car accident. Monitors were blaring, nurses zigzagging from bed to bed, families hunched in clusters in the waiting areas, faces pinched with fatigue.

I scanned a patient chart, scribbling notes. The patient was stable, everything was on track. I was on my way out, already halfway down the hall, when I saw her.

Harper sat in a family room, knees squared, her body angled toward a woman who looked like she hadn't slept for days. The woman's eyes were rimmed red, hands tearing a tissue into thin strips. Harper didn't lean in; she kept her posture open, but not soft.

I stopped just outside, where I could watch without being obvious.

"No one's saying anything! No one will tell me what's happening," the woman said. "He's my father. I have a right to know."

"I'm going to get those answers for you," said Harper, "but there may not be a good answer right now."

"You can't tell me he's going to be okay."

"I can't make promises about outcomes, and no one should. What I can tell you is that the team is watching him closely, and if his condition changes, you'll be updated immediately."

"That's what they said yesterday."

"And I'm saying it again because it's still true." Harper didn't blink. "That's the only honest answer I can give you right now."

The woman's shoulders caved in. She looked past Harper, focused somewhere over her shoulder.

"I don't know what to do," she said. "What do I even do right now?"

"You can ask questions. You can get updates from the nurse every few hours. Make sure we have the right contact information for you." Harper waited a beat. "And you can take a break. Go grab coffee. Step outside, get some air. You've been here since yesterday afternoon."

"I don't want to leave in case something happens."

"His nurse and doctor agree he's serious but stable. If anything changes, we'll call you. I promise."

The woman nodded, slow. Not really convinced, but not frantic either.

Harper stood, then put an arm around the woman's shoulder. "Let's check in with the nursing team and make sure they know you're waiting for updates. If you need me, you can reach me through the main desk."

"Okay." The woman wiped her eyes. "Thank you."

Harper walked her right past me. I watched them go, then turned back for the surgical wing.

An hour later, I spotted Harper talking to an attending I recognized, just outside the OR by the nurses' station. He was in the middle of explaining something, hands flying as he talked, but Harper only listened, arms crossed and face unreadable.

Whatever she said next, it made him falter mid-sentence, head dropping, and then he nodded, slow, like he was swallowing a pill and didn't like the taste.

Harper's reply was clipped, and then she stepped around him. I caught up with him at the elevator, tapped his elbow.

"Stephens. You good?

He shot me a look, face flushed and twisted into a scowl so deep it looked like Harper had pressed it in by hand. "I'm fuckin' sick of admin always down here, just waiting to make us look bad."

I chuckled. "What she call you out on?"

He shook his head. "I told the patient I'd have a test result for them tomorrow. I mean, yeah, tests can take longer, but who cares if it keeps them off my back?"

I frowned, the answer obvious. "Families treat your word like gospel. And if Harper checking you annoys you? Man, wait until Webb gets in your ass when it goes up the chain."

He arched a brow, a sneer in his voice. "Yeah? Like that death a few weeks ago?"

"You heard about that?"

He scoffed, pushing the elevator button. "What, are you new? Nothing's a secret around here, Vaughn." He watched the numbers light up. "Sutton's not wrong, I guess. It's just not that big a deal."

The elevator dinged and he stepped in.

"It's not that big a deal," I echoed, "until it is."

The doors slid shut. I had a department meeting in fifteen minutes. I had notes to write and patients to check in on. Any of those tasks would have been a better use of headspace.

Instead, I was thinking about Harper Sutton. Wondering if she was always that direct with staff, or if there was something about our conversation—and my situation—that she'd decided would be different.

* * *

Later that evening, Jasmine Keller, an ICU nurse, walked into the break room where I'd been catching up on my internet surfing.

She appeared to be surprised to see me; a smile spread across her lips. She poured herself a cup of coffee and leaned against the counter, her smile settling into a smug grin.

"Nurse Keller," I said, from my seat at a round table .

"Dr. Vaughn. What's uh...what's up?"

"You tell me. You look like you're busting at the seams with...something."

"Uh, so did you know the day shift nurses have a group chat? And you're a frequent topic?"

My head tilted. "Excuse me?"

She sauntered across the room and pulled out a chair at my table. She settled into it, then leaned in. "The name of the chat changes depending on which part of your body they're obsessed with. I can't tell you what last week's chat was called, but this week it's *Dr. Vaughn's Forearms*. It's a whole situation."

She sipped her coffee, painting on an innocent expression though her eyes were laughing.

"Jasmine, what the hell are you saying?"

"You've never seen how they stare at you? They're not very good at hiding it. You rolled your sleeves up during a consult last week and Karina almost tipped a crash cart trying to look."

If I could, I'd be blushing. "Jesus, Jas. I didn't really need to know that."

"I'm just saying. You've got adoring fans." She studied me over the rim of her cup as she casually sipped, then added, "But that's not why I'm glad I ran into you."

I locked my phone and slid it into a pocket. "There's more?"

"You've been on this floor a lot today. Hovering."

I squinted, confused. "I'm down here all the time. This is where trauma patients are."

"Mmmmm." She smiled. "The group chat reports your eyes have been following Harper Sutton."

My brows rose, but I said nothing.

"This is new behavior, Cole. One of the things the nurses notice is that you don't pay anyone dust. You come in, you do your job, you get out. It makes them feel like you don't favor one over the other, so there's no hate or competition for attention. You feel me?"

I shrugged. "So now there's hate and competition? Because I've been working?"

"We both know you're a smart man, Dr. Vaughn. You been circling this floor like a vulture. And I want you to know I see you."

Jasmine pushed off the table and stood, toting her cup with her. "I'm not judging. Just fair warning. Harper isn't like the nurses who giggle when you walk by, who might have dreams of bagging a handsome doctor."

"Watch it—my mother did that exact thing."

"And I'm sure her husband is an amazing man, like his son. And I want his *son* to know that Harper Sutton is not someone to play with."

"I'm not *playing* with anyone."

"Good. Harper doesn't need any distractions. And you —" She pointed at me, playfully smirking, "can be very distracting when you want to be."

"But I'm not trying to distract anyone, Jas."

"Oh, you sweet summer child. It's cute how naive you are." She winked, then headed for the door, then stopped. "You don't have to try to be distracting, Cole. You just are."

Then she walked out of the room.

Well. That was interesting.

I checked my phone. No new messages, nothing that demanded my presence in this building. No fires to put out other than the apparent slow burn of the nurses at each other's throats.

I cut through the corridor to my office, grabbed my bag, shrugged into my jacket and fished out my keys, then slipped out the side door and took the stairs to the parking garage.

The place was desolate. My footsteps echoed, joined by the drone of the sodium lights. Halfway to my car, the crash of glass meeting concrete rang out, followed by a hissing "Shit!"

I turned toward the sound. Harper stood by her car, staring down at her phone—or what was left of it. The screen looked like a windshield after a head-on collision. Spiderwebbed, black and glinting.

"Need a hand?" I called.

She looked up. "Not sure there's anything you can do for this, Dr. Vaughn."

"DOA," I quipped, cringing. "That's not the phone my number's in, is it?"

"Nah. This is my work phone. Brand new, too. I've only had this thing a few days."

I walked closer, drawn like a moth. "Three days? And you're out here raw doggin' it with no case?"

She thumbed the power button. No response. "I've been busy."

"Rough day?"

"Long day. Long week." She slumped against her car, a late model Lexus. "At least now I have an ironclad excuse to ignore Dr. Rice for the next day or so."

Her gaze locked on mine. "I would have thought you'd escaped for the day already."

"Could say the same about you. Your work ethic suggests ain't nobody at home waiting for you."

"Bold, coming from a man who's also just leaving work."

We laughed, then fell into silence for a beat. Somewhere, a car alarm yipped, then fell quiet.

"I saw you today," I told her.

"Saw me where?" she asked, dropping the dead phone into her bag.

"In the ICU. With the woman who was asking about her father and didn't want to leave. You were good with her."

Harper's expression shifted, a ripple of compassion beneath the surface. "Well, it's the job."

"Yeah, but a lot of people do that job differently than you do."

She laughed, pushing off her car. "A lot of people in my job are trying not to get the hospital sued."

"True," I said, conceding with a nod. "But most people in your job have a few standard phrases they keep in their pocket, then offer a pat on the shoulder and walk off. You seem to really care about the family, about the patient. Even that doc you yelled at today. Stephens–"

"I did not yell at him," she interrupted. "I said he needed to stop trying to be a hero. He makes my job harder when the family comes to my office saying Dr. Stephens said this thing and it didn't happen."

"I get that. But I'm just saying–I'm trying to compliment you. Damn."

A bubble of laughter spilled from her. I really liked the sound.

"Thank you," she said when she caught her breath. "I'm fired up. I need a drink."

"Now you're speaking my language," I said before I could stop myself. "Where you planning to get one?"

"You know Rafferty's? On Fifth? It's more of a lounge that serves wings, beer, finger food. But there's no loud music and they have huge TVs to air a game or...whatever."

"Sounds like a nice spot. Would you welcome some company? Or..." Feeling embarrassed now, I tried to backtrack. "I mean, if you wanted to be alone, that's cool. I don't mean to horn in on your Me Time or whatever."

She pulled out her key fob and pressed a button. Her car turned on, the lights illuminating.

"I'm headed to Rafferty's to pick out a table. Do with that info whatever you like."

She slid into her car then. Her tail lights flared and I stepped back so she could pull out. I watched her thread down the ramp, red lights vanishing into the shadows.

Then I raced to my car, pulled out, and headed toward Fifth Street.

Chapter Five

HARPER

I slid into my usual booth in the back of Rafferty's. The place was busier than I'd expected it to be, which was fine. I liked a crowd thick enough that two colleagues having drinks wouldn't draw a glance, but not so loud that we'd have to shout to be heard.

Rafferty's didn't pretend to be anything it wasn't. It had an urban edge but was upscale, a perfect balance of grit and polish. Concrete floors gleamed underfoot and exposed ductwork ran overhead. The tables were thick slabs of reclaimed wood, each one catching the glow of Edison bulbs dangling above.

The bar itself stretched long, a fusion of steel and wood, the shelves behind it crowded with small-batch spirits and local brews. Flat screens were generously hung and looped sports highlights with the sound dialed way down.

A waiter materialized at my table, order pad already in hand. "Welcome to Rafferty's. What can I get started for you tonight?"

"I'll take a whiskey sour."

I pulled out my personal phone while I waited. Three texts from Alicia—random chitchat and asking me how I was doing. One from Mom about Sunday dinner and if I could pick up a bottle of wine on my way. And one from my brother, Aaron. He was the only boy, so though he was divorced and had a child, he was spoiled, even at thirty-one.

I opened the text, curious. He rarely reached out unless he needed something.

AARON:

Hey Harpy.

Mia has a school dance coming up and I agreed to take her shopping. Any chance you could tag along? You got a style that I like and she'll listen to you about what she should get.

I grinned at his crass nickname for me, then at the thought of shopping with my niece. I happily texted that I would join them on their shopping trip—just name the date and the place; Auntie will be on the way.

My shattered work phone sat in the bottom of my bag, a small disaster that I wasn't looking forward to reporting. I pulled it out, examining the destroyed screen. The IT department was going to have a field day.

So was Rowan. This was the second phone I'd had to replace lately.

My drink arrived, condensation already beading on the glass. I thanked the waiter and took a sip, tartness making me wince slightly before the warmth of the bourbon spread through my chest. I sighed, trying to remember the last time I'd done this. Just gone out for drinks on a weeknight, no agenda, and enjoyed myself.

The door swung open, spilling a chill into the room. Cole stepped inside, his gaze moving over the crowd. It only took a second for him to spot me. His lips curled into a smile as he made his way toward the booth.

"Wasn't sure you'd actually show," I said as he slid in across from me.

"Wasn't sure you actually wanted me to." He settled in, comfortable. "You did drive off pretty fast."

"I was giving you time to decide."

"Appreciate it." He lifted a hand, caught the waiter's eye. "Bourbon. Neat."

When we were alone again, I gestured at my destroyed phone on the table. "Exhibit A in why my brother, the tech pro, calls me a walking disaster."

Cole picked it up, turned it over. "It only took you three days to kill it, huh? Didn't IT give you a case?"

"Yes," I admitted. "I don't know where I put it. I've been busy."

"Too busy to order one? Don't you have an assistant that could get one for you?"

I scowled, becoming overly concerned with my whiskey sour. "They're also very busy. They've got important things to do."

"Do I want to ask how you destroyed the last one?"

I laughed despite myself. "Uh, I dropped it in a pot of chili?"

"Oh. Oh shit." Cole's laugh was deep and rich, even at my expense. "How does someone even do that? Were you cooking and texting?"

"So what if I was?"

Cole raised an eyebrow, leaning back in the booth. "I'm just picturing you in an apron, stirring chili with one hand, negotiating with the other, and then..."

"It was less dramatic than that. It fell right through my fingers. By the time Aaron fished it out of the pot, it was gone."

The server set his drink down in front of him; he took a sip, then relaxed, sinking into the supple brown leather. His gaze flicked over the room, taking it all in.

"Sounds like we've had the same week," he said after a long pause.

"Not quite. I'm not a surgeon. But pretty much."

"So, how does this roll out from your side?"

I filled him in, from Dr. Rice gearing up for a fight to the careful language everyone was using, to trying to stay ahead of a situation that kept shifting under my feet. He listened, nodding like he was interested, not just waiting for his turn to talk.

"The way I see it? They're scared," he said when I finished.

"Terrified," I agreed. "Which makes them dangerous. Are you?"

"No. But yes. If that makes sense."

My head tilted at that. I understood, actually. But I wanted him to say more.

"Off the record, right?" he asked.

When I nodded, he continued.

"I'm confident in my skills. I wouldn't have an MD, I wouldn't make people call me doctor, I wouldn't be cutting people open if I wasn't. I'm also confident I did everything right. I gotta be, you know?"

My head bobbed in a deep nod. Because if anything went wrong, he would be the first person under scrutiny.

"So, if I'm Dr. Stephens, this is getting swept under the rug, I'm sure. As a Black American surgeon?" He paused, lifted and lowered his shoulders in a shrug, then picked up his bourbon and took a slow sip, curling his tongue out to lick his lip afterward.

God, that was hot.

"That's got to be annoying. I mean, I know it's annoying."

"I was warned about it, on my way up." He smiled without humor. "I always expect lots of questions phrased as concern. So yeah, I'm not scared about my actions. I'm scared about how I'll be perceived."

"You've seen this before."

"Enough times to know how it can end."

Bar noise filled the space between our lapses in conversation—laughter from the corner booth, sports commentary from the TVs, the clink of glasses.

"So, how long have you been at Ridgeway?" Cole asked.

"Nine years. You?"

"Three. I came from a trauma fellowship in Baltimore."

"Baltimore. Big Fun." I grinned, hoping he'd catch the joke. He smiled, so he did. "So what brought you to Ridgeway? We're considerably smaller."

"A good program trumps working at a big, busy hospital. Level one trauma center, solid teaching opportunities. I wanted to build something in a spot where I could get comfortable."

He took another sip before asking, "What about you? Where were you before?"

"I worked in case management at a smaller hospital. I was recruited for a patient advocacy role, then promoted to risk management, then director over both since they often cross over."

"You like it? I mean...you're good at it."

I thought about that. "You're right. I'm good at it."

"But...?"

I smiled. "But nothing. Most days, I like being able to help families navigate the system. I like fixing problems before they become lawsuits. I like making things work."

"And the other days?"

"The other days I realize I'm just making the machine run the same way it's always run, instead of changing how it runs." I caught myself. "Sorry. Shop talk can get ranty."

"I mean, it's all relative. It got honest." He leaned forward, drawing his arms around his glass, clasping his long, well-manicured fingers together. "You really think you don't bring change?"

"I think I can change small things. Communication. Process. How we talk to families." I met his eyes. "But the big stuff? The things that make the small stuff necessary in the first place? Those don't change."

"That's why you're good at your job. You see the system clearly. You don't waste your time on shit you can't do anything about."

"Or maybe I'm just cynical."

"Those aren't mutually exclusive."

I snorted—a real, undignified laugh. He had a point. No lies detected.

"Harper?"

I looked up slowly, as if surfacing from deep water. Jeremiah stood next to the booth, a black sweater stretching across broad shoulders. My stomach did a neat little free fall, the drop you get when the elevator starts to move before you're ready.

I pasted a smile on my lips. "Jeremiah. Nice to see you."

He smiled back, but it didn't quite reach his eyes. "You were going to text me about that supper club thing."

"I'm sorry, I meant to update you. It has been a busy week."

"Yeah. Uh..." He slipped his hands into the pockets of his jeans. His gaze shifted to Cole, curious but cautious. "I figured work was kicking your ass. Saw you over here and wanted to make sure you were good."

"I am."

His eyes flicked to Cole again, then back to me. The question was obvious even if he didn't ask it.

"Oh! This is Dr. Vaughn," I said. "He's a surgeon at RMC. Cole, this is Jeremiah. He's a project manager for a tech firm downtown."

Cole nodded. "What's up?"

"'Sup." Jeremiah's tone was cool. He looked at me again. "Well, I'll let you get back to your drinks."

"Jeremiah—"

"No, it's cool. Really." He stepped back. "Just, you know. Maybe give me a heads-up next time if you're going dark. So I know you're alive."

"Excuse me?" My brows shot nearly to my hairline. "A heads-up? On going dark?"

"Next thing I know, you're hugged up wit' a surgeon nigga from your job—"

"Whoa, Jeremiah..." I held up a hand because what in the *Fatal Attraction* was happening here? "Could we chat later instead of doing this right here? Right now? Because I promise you will not get the result you desire if you keep going down this track."

After a few moments of a tense standoff, his shoulders dropped and his chin lifted. "Nah," he bit out. "I see where I stand. Don't worry about calling me about shit."

I watched him go, then glanced over at Cole, who hadn't said a word. His lips pressed together, his eyes tracking mine, full of unspoken questions.

"That was not what he was trying to make it look like. We are—were *very* casual." I curled my fingers around my drink, let the glass cool my palm.

"Oh. Okay. So a cut-buddy type of thing."

I shot him a look over the rim of my glass. "If the term 'cut-buddy' is what we call having our urges satisfied on a loose schedule?" I took a sip, the bite fizzling out at the edges. My face was in flames. "Yes. That."

"Uh huh." He nodded, slowly. I watched his tongue roll across his teeth under thick, juicy lips. "Forgot to set up your next sneaky link?"

"Cole. If you don't..." I giggled, halfway embarrassed by his bare-bones assessment of my situation with Jeremiah. Damn if the man wasn't right, though. "I told him the day this case came in that my life was about to be very busy. And that I would let him know if I was interested in going out. It completely slipped my mind."

I met his eyes. "Does that make me terrible?"

"Makes you human." He took a long sip of his drink, then set his glass down. "Though, his understanding of the relationship does not match yours. That, or he was hoping it would be a friends-to-lovers type of situation."

"Not me getting caught up in some fuck-buddy-to-bae thing. Isn't that how it always is? One of them is pining, hanging in the cut, taking the scraps and hoping the other will catch feelings?"

"Well-versed in the tropes and matters of the heart," Cole said, laughter dancing in his eyes. "Sounds like you have some experience."

"A little," I confirmed, thinking about the last man I'd hoped to be entangled with.

He played with my feelings, let me fall hard for him, led me to believe I was the one for him. Took me to meet this Mama. Then a week later, began to detach.

I heard rumors of him being seen around town with a tall, thick, gorgeous social media maven with great assets. When I confronted him, he said everything I'd thought I'd had was in my head. He hadn't promised anything to me, so there was nothing to fulfill or feel bad about.

We'd had something, or so I thought. Then I learned we'd had nothing. Like I'd imagined the entire relationship.

"Let's just say I've officially been on both sides of the equation" Eager to take the glare of the spotlight off of me, I asked, "How about you? We briefly discussed you not having anyone waiting for you at home."

"Aye don't take your frustrations out on me," he shot back, a little grin poking at the edges of his mouth.

"I'm not. I'm just being nosy, now that you met my boy toy in the most awkward way possible."

Cole laughed. "Fair enough. No, I'm not seeing anyone right now. Haven't been for a while."

"Why not? You seem like a decent catch. Handsome, educated, good job..."

"Work," he replied, as I assumed he would. "It's always work. Sixty, seventy-hour weeks don't leave time for playing with dating apps or meeting people the old-fashioned way."

"And when you do have time?"

He traced the rim of his glass with his index finger, contemplating. "People love the idea of dating a doctor," he said, "until they realize what it actually means. Missed calls when emergencies happen. Birthdays spent in the OR.

Vacations cut short. Rescheduled dates. Never being able to guarantee you'll be somewhere at a specific time."

Cole paused, taking another sip. "And that's before you add being a Black professional in this field."

"Stress on stress," I agreed with a nod. "The hours alone would kill most relationships."

"For sure. Then there's the expectations. Everyone assumes you're rich the moment you say *surgeon*, but they don't see the student loans or the years of living on ramen during residency."

Cole finished his bourbon with one last swallow, sliding the glass to the edge of the table. "Dating other doctors is its own special level of hell. Imagine two headstrong people, both trying to be the alpha, both of them always the smartest person in the room?"

He blew out a breath, puffing his cheeks. "I like a woman who challenges me, makes me see something in a different way. I just don't want to be in competition all the time."

I nodded, thinking of all the hospital romances I'd witnessed crash and burn. "If I'm being honest, though, I have to hope that saying can be true—if we want to, we will. Otherwise, it'd be like admitting there's no one out there for you. Or me. And that just can't be true."

"That's a good way to look at it," Cole said. Then he pointed, jabbing a finger in my face. "See? You're good at this shit."

I shrugged, taking the compliment. "So why trauma surgery?" I asked. "That's got to be intense."

"It is. But it's also the clearest that medicine gets. Someone's hurt, you fix them. It's skill and brain power and speed and whether you've got what it takes to save a life. Right now."

"And do you?"

"Most days?" He considered the question, bobbing his head side to side. "Yeah. Some days I am That Nigga. I can't afford to think I'm not. Some days, it doesn't matter how smart or skilled or fast you are."

I heard what he wasn't saying. The thing we were both dancing around, the investigation that trailed him like a shadow he couldn't shake.

"Cole," I leaned in, my tone barely above a whisper.

"Harper." He matched my posture, his deep brown eyes focused on my face and nothing else.

"Why'd you meet me here?"

He was quiet for a moment, then said, "I've been going home alone to an empty house and letting myself overthink. There is such a thing as too much alone time. Having an actual conversation with someone who gets it sounded good to me."

"That's it?"

"Well, you didn't object when I suggested I join you. And you're nice to talk to, after passing each other in the hallways at RMC. I wanted to know if the you I saw in the ICU was who you actually are or if that was variations on a performance."

"What do you mean? Which me?"

"With the family and with Stephens. You switched up on him real fast. Got in his ass. He was not happy about it."

I felt my lips quirk into a smile. "That's an accurate summary of his feelings on our encounter. Ask me if I give a fuck. He needs to stop playing hero."

"See?" He grinned. "That's what I wanted to know—if you're the same person in the waiting room and the parking garage and at this table."

"I'm betting I'm not."

"Hayull naw," he drawled. "I like Rafferty's Harper a lot. *A lot* a lot."

I didn't know what to do with that, so I drained the last of my drink.

"What about you?" Cole asked. "Why'd you invite me to join you?"

"Same reasons, I guess. I wanted to see if you were as..." I paused, mostly for drama.

"As..." His brows rose, curious.

"*Competent* off-script."

"Competent." He pretended to choke. "That's how you describe me?"

"It's a compliment, Dr. Vaughn."

"Uh-huh. I'm about to go home and think of some bland, beige compliments for you. You're efficient. Pleasant. What you say to that?"

"I say thank you, can I have another?"

The bartender bellowed last call from the bar. I glanced at my watch.

"Last call? It's like..." Cole picked up his phone. "A quarter to ten?"

"Rafferty's closes at ten," I told him. "It's truly a lounge for washed people."

"A'ight," he said, giving a signal to our waiter. "I'll pick up the tab. It's the competent thing to do."

"Lord. Like competent isn't the highest praise coming from hospital administration."

The waiter dropped off the check. Cole slipped his credit card into the leather folio without glancing at the total.

"You know," I said, watching him, "I wonder if we shouldn't make a habit of this."

"Of what? Having drinks?"

"At a bar. Just the two of us." I gestured between us. "You're part of an active investigation. I'm supposed to be impartial."

Cole leaned back, studying me. "Is that the only reason?"

Nope, I thought. I was definitely going to go home, pull my vibrator out from my drawer, and stroke myself to a sweaty orgasm while replaying every second of this encounter.

I didn't say that, though. And he didn't press for an answer.

The waiter returned the folio. Cole slid his card back into his wallet, then stepped out of the booth. "I'll walk you out."

The parking lot was cold and mostly empty. We walked side by side, not talking, but it felt comfortable instead of awkward.

I unlocked the car, turning to say goodnight. Cole was closer than I expected. Not crowding, just...there.

"Whether or not we do this again—and I hope we do because those people don't scare me—I'm glad you invited me out. I needed normal conversation with another human. I forget what that feels like."

"Same." I opened my car door, one foot inside. "And you're right. We should definitely do this again."

"I'd ask you to text me when you get home but..." He started to laugh.

"See, you don't listen, Dr. Vaughn. You're in my *personal* phone, not my work phone."

"Then I'll expect a text when you make it home." He stepped back. "Drive safe, Harper."

"You too, Cole."

I watched him walk toward his car in my rearview mirror. He lifted a hand in a small wave before getting in.

The drive home was quiet, just the hum of the road and my thoughts. I'd enjoyed that, more than I'd expected to. Cole was easy to talk to, easier to laugh with. Thoughtful, deep, intellectual in a way that didn't need to prove itself. Honest without oversharing.

And yes, *fine*. In a way I was trying hard not to overthink.

At home, I pulled out my phone and texted Cole the minute I crossed the threshold into my apartment. Then I put myself through my normal routine—keys in the bowl, bag on the chair, phone on the charger.

I headed to my bathroom, washed my makeup off, and pulled off my clothes, dumping my suit into a dry cleaning bag.

I checked my phone one more time before hopping in the shower.

Cole:

Thanks for letting me know you made it home.

COLE:

See you tomorrow. Sleep well, Harper.

I set the phone down and sighed. Here comes real life, encroaching on my fantasies of fucking that fine ass surgeon until I couldn't see or walk straight.

Chapter Six

COLE

"Patient is a twenty-six-year-old male."

My intern's eyes darted between me and the bedside computer screen as if he hoped I wouldn't notice the gaps in his presentation. "Motorcycle versus SUV. Uh—patient presented with blunt force trauma to the chest and abdomen. GCS was fourteen on scene, dropped to eleven during transport. Initial CT showed a grade three splenic laceration. Possible liver involvement, but radiology couldn't confirm without contrast."

Martin let the last words hang. I watched sweat bead along his hairline. His hands trembled slightly as he held the tablet in front of him like a shield. He was young and had a fresh-from-medical-school eagerness that made him volunteer to present cases even when he clearly had not prepared adequately.

Behind him, three other interns hovered in the hallway outside the ICU, watching the scene play out like they were witnessing an execution.

"Is that it?" I asked.

"Oh. Uhm. Hemoglobin on arrival was...nine point two," Martin continued. "We started two units of packed red cells and he has been stable. Vitals are holding. Blood pressure is one-fifteen over seventy, heart rate is ninety-two, respiratory rate is eighteen on room air."

I let the silence stretch for a beat. Then another. Martin's confidence started to crumble around the edges.

"Hemoglobin was nine point two when?" I asked.

"Uhm..." Martin blinked. "On arrival."

"What time was that measurement taken?"

He glanced down at the chart, fumbling with the tablet. "Oh-three-hundred hours," he answered quietly.

"And what time is it now?"

He looked at his watch. His Adam's apple bobbed when he swallowed. "Seven fifteen."

"So why do I give a shit about that number?" I asked. "Your patient has a grade three laceration. He's losing blood. You presented based on labs from four hours ago, so you don't know if his hemoglobin is stable, dropping, or crashing."

I kept my volume level but firm. I did not need to yell to make my point clear. Rounds were a time to learn, and sometimes learning looked like a reprimand.

"So what should you have done before report?"

Martin's face went pale. "I should have checked recent labs first."

"You should have checked recent labs first," I parroted. "Dr. Martin, if your patient is bleeding into his abdomen and you're presenting to me based on outdated information, what does that tell me about your understanding of trauma as a practice area?"

"That I don't understand it well enough, sir."

"You don't understand it well enough *yet*." I looked at the other residents, all of whom suddenly found the floor interesting. "Anyone else want to present a trauma patient without current vital information? We've got time to waste in the ICU, right?"

Three heads shook in unison. Nobody made eye contact.

"No, of course not. Martin, get current labs and a repeat abdominal exam. If his hemoglobin has dropped below eight or if there is any change, I want to know. Then we will talk about whether we are taking him to the OR. The rest of you, I want updates on your patients in one hour, and I want those updates to include data that's less than thirty minutes old. Go."

They scattered like I had fired a starting gun. I watched them disappear down the hallway, then pulled out my phone to check the time. Seven seventeen. Morning rounds on Friday always ran long because the interns' brains were already on weekend time.

I pocketed the phone and headed down the hall. I had three post-operative patients from earlier in the week who needed checking, and if Martin's trauma patient was still bleeding, I would need to schedule an emergency splenectomy.

Two nurses at the main station had been talking, heads bent close together in a conspiratorial way that meant they were discussing something they did not want overheard. The conversation stopped the instant they saw me. One of them, a younger woman whose name I could not recall, smiled at me. The other, Karina, actually blushed and looked down at the computer screen in front of her.

I nodded at them and kept walking toward the computer station near bed three. I logged in and pulled up his chart. Vitals were stable, blood pressure was holding, heart rate had come down slightly. Oxygen saturation was ninety-eight percent.

I walked to the bedside. The patient had a full sleeve of tattoos visible on his right arm where the hospital gown did not cover. His eyes were closed. I did a quick physical exam. His abdomen was tender when I palpated the left upper quadrant, but it was not rigid. Bowel sounds were present.

"Dr. Vaughn?"

I turned to find Karina in the doorway, her dark hair hiding under a surgical cap. She was holding a tablet close to her chest.

"Yes?"

"Dr. Martin asked me to let you know the labs are ready for his patient."

"Thanks." I swung to the nearest computer and pulled them up. Hemoglobin was eight point eight; down from nine point two, but not catastrophically low. "Could you page Dr. Martin and tell him if hemoglobin drops below eight, start another unit and call me immediately? And someone needs to check him again in four hours."

"Will do," she said with a smile. I gave her an appreciative nod. Karina had been working in the ICU for five years, making her more valuable than half the residents on any given day.

Which was why it was odd that she just...stood there. Usually, the nurses hurried away after getting instructions. Lingering wasn't part of the ICU routine—there was too much to do.

"Nurse?" I prompted, half-turning from the computer screen. "Was there something else?"

She startled slightly, as if she'd drifted and only now snapped back. "No—sorry," she said, then smiled. It was a different smile than I was used to. Softer. Almost shy. "Have a good day, Dr. Vaughn."

I stared at the empty doorway, trying to figure out what had just happened. Karina had never smiled at me like that before. This was new.

Or it wasn't, and I had been completely oblivious to it until Jasmine pointed out the group chat.

I finished checking my other post-operative patients. All of them were stable and boring, which was exactly how you wanted post-operative patients to be. I signed off on discharge orders for two of them, wrote a note about weaning sedation on the third, and got out of the ICU as quickly as I could without looking like I was running away.

In the hallway, I passed two more nurses I recognized from the night shift. They both looked at me, then they looked at each other. Then one of them giggled.

Giggled. What the fuck?

I ducked into the stairwell and yanked out my phone.

ME:

Tell me something, Jas. Did I grow a second head overnight or is everyone acting weird?

The response came back almost immediately.

JASMINE:

No, baby. You're finally noticing something that's been happening a long time.

I shoved the phone back in my pocket and took the

stairs down to the second floor. Only one person could make this day better.

She was coming straight at me, long strides eating up the hallway like she had places to be. Her camel-colored suit was tailored to her frame, with heels that added at least three inches to her height. Her hair was pulled back, a few strands escaping to frame her face. She had a tablet tucked in her elbow, phone pressed tight to her ear.

From the outside, Harper was the full package: professional, polished, untouchable. Queen of the conference room.

But I'd already met the Harper who laughed at my jokes over drinks.

"I hear you, and I get that, Samuel," she was saying into the phone, her tone clipped. "But an assessment is required and that means I need access to the complete file, not the sanitized version you're comfortable sharing."

After a pause, she rolled her eyes and huffed. "I'm not just *anybody*, Sam. I'm administration. I need the complete—"

Her eyes found mine and her expression instantly morphed. The mask slipped and I saw the same thing I was feeling—the urge to rush over and give her a hug and crack some inside jokes.

"You need some time to send my request up the chain. I'll call you back," she said, then hung up before they could say a word and came to a stop a few feet away from me. "Dr. Vaughn."

"Ms. Sutton."

I eyed the phone in her hand. It was a different model than she'd used the night before. "Looks like you got a replacement phone already. With a case."

Her lips twitched in her attempt not to smile. "It's a

loaner. My new phone and case are on the way, though. How are you?"

"I'm, uh..." I glanced around. Two nurses at a nearby station were definitely watching us. I recognized one of them from this morning. She wasn't even pretending not to stare. "I'm fine. How is your morning so far?"

"Bureaucratic," Harper said, shifting the tablet to her other hand. "I shouldn't have to beg for files but here I am, begging for files."

"At least you didn't spend the morning with interns who forget that trauma patients can bleed to death while you're presenting old labs that tell you nothing about the patient's current status."

"Oh." She winced. "I want nothing to do with that."

"Yeah, I don't blame you. I don't want anything to do with it either."

I wanted to keep talking. Actually, I wanted to ask her if she'd been thinking about last night, if she'd replayed the conversation in her head the way I had or if I'd blown it out of proportion.

But we were standing in the middle of a hospital corridor, people streaming past, nurses pretending not to listen but catching every word.

Instead, I asked, "You headed somewhere?"

"I have a meeting in about twelve minutes." Harper glanced at her watch, then back at me. "Walk and talk?"

We fell into step together. Harper was tall enough in her heels that I didn't have to slow my pace to match hers. She walked close enough to me that I caught her scent, that same vanilla and something warmer that I had noticed last night.

"So who's making you beg for files?"

"Legal. They started putting up barricades the minute I

asked for a complete patient history. They like to preach about proper channels, but we all know they don't want to hand over anything. Ever."

"Do they know who they're dealing with?"

Harper grinned, her face brightening. "They're learning."

We walked past the cafeteria entrance. The smells of burnt coffee and steam table food drifted out. A few people glanced at us as we passed—two professionals walking together, nothing unusual about it, except I was hyperaware of how it looked for Harper and me to be walking side by side.

"So, you got big Friday night plans?" I asked, trying to sound casual.

She looked over. A note of curiosity, nothing more. "Tonight? Probably just go home, catch up on *Reasonable Doubt*. Why?"

"That's your Friday night plan? Just going home?"

"What's wrong with that?"

"I mean, it sounds kind of depressing."

Harper laughed, a short, dry sound. "Or relaxing after a long week. You're saying you have more exciting plans?"

"No, actually. I'm going to do the exact same thing," I admitted. "I'll probably go home, eat something out of a container, watch whatever's on TV until I fall asleep on the couch."

She gave me a look, her lips twisting. "I was at least going to cook. Your version sounds bleak."

"It does." I held the door open for her as we turned into the next corridor. "You want to save me from that?"

Harper stopped cold. We were near the elevators now, people flowing around us like water around rocks. She studied me for a long moment, her expression unreadable.

"Are you asking me to have dinner with you, Dr. Vaughn?"

"I am. Somewhere that's not a lounge that closes at ten. Where we could talk without a last call."

She didn't answer right away. I could see her working it over, turning it around in her mind, a flicker of caution crossing her face.

"You do realize this is a terrible idea," she said finally. "If anyone finds out—"

"Then we'll deal with it." I watched her, holding my ground. "My life doesn't stop because some people have questions. I'd like to have dinner with you. Away from all this."

"What time?"

Relief washed over me. "Seven? Seven thirty? I can pick you up or we can meet—"

"Let's meet. Less complicated that way." Her phone buzzed. She glanced at it and grimaced. "That's my five-minute warning."

"Go. I'll text you the details."

She started to walk away, then turned back. "Make it somewhere nice."

"I got this."

She disappeared around the corner toward the administrative wing, hips moving in a rhythm that made my pulse jump. As soon as she was gone, I pulled out my phone and immediately started searching for restaurants.

Chapter Seven

COLE

The interior at Provisions was warm and inviting—walls papered in thick cream, soft pendant lighting, tables dressed in ivory linens and cloth napkins. Large windows along the front let in what was left of the waning sunlight. Potted plants lined the windowsills and hung from the ceiling in the corners. The open kitchen meant diners at the bar could watch the chefs working, and the noise level was energetic but not loud.

I gave the hostess my name and she led me through the dining room to a table near the back corner. It was a two-top with a candle flickering in a small glass holder, positioned far enough from the kitchen that we would be able to talk without competing with the sound of pots and pans.

Harper was already there.

She wore jeans that hugged her hips and a rust-colored

silk blouse with a deep V-neck that showed off her collarbone and the hollow at the base of her throat. Her hair was down tonight, shoulder-length curls framing her face in a wash-and-go style. She was absorbed in her phone, scrolling with one thumb, but she looked up as I came closer.

I slid into the chair across from her, the wood sighing beneath me. "Hey. You been here long?"

"Maybe five minutes." She set her phone face-down on the table. "I ordered wine. I hope that's okay."

"More than okay," I said.

As if he had been waiting for that cue, our server appeared with a bottle and two glasses. He poured wine into both glasses as he introduced himself and the specials, then asked, "Can I get you started with any appetizers?"

Harper ordered scallops; I went with the short rib on special. Our waiter, Derek, disappeared into the background with promises to bring bread shortly.

"To Friday," said Harper, lifting her glass in a toast.

"To Friday," I agreed, clinking my glass against hers.

The wine was good. I was not a wine person—I usually drank bourbon or beer—but I could appreciate a good red.

Harper tilted her head, eyes narrowing slightly as she studied me across the table. "There's something different about you tonight."

I laughed. "It's the company. But I'm also distracted by this thing going on at RMC. Today was strange."

"What kind of strange are we talking about?"

I swirled my wine, getting into the story. "So apparently, I've been oblivious to this group chat that some of the staff have. In this group chat, they discuss..." I paused, still not believing I was saying this out loud. "Various topics, including but not limited to my forearms."

Harper blinked, her lips parting in surprise before she

started to laugh. "I'm sorry, I'm not laughing at you. I'm just...your face right now. Your forearms?"

"There's an entire conversation in a group text about my forearms. Also, the chat name changes every week based on whatever part of my body they are fixated on."

Harper's face went through several expressions in rapid succession. She pressed her hand over her mouth, but I saw her shoulders shaking. "Cole!" she squeaked. "Stop. Are you serious?"

"Completely serious. One of the nurses said she couldn't tell me what last week's obsession was. I don't even want to know."

Harper's burst of laughter made her lean back in her chair. Her laugh was infectious, and I found myself smiling despite my embarrassment.

"I can guess. It's below the waist—"

"Harper, I really—"

"I'm sorry. I don't mean to embarrass you, it's just... that's the funniest thing I've heard all year."

"I heard humiliation builds character."

"It's not humiliation. It's..." She paused, flurrying her hands around. "It's people being people. You know this is completely normal, right?"

"Normal?"

"Normal! Like any workplace, hospital staff have group chats about everyone. The cute residents, the difficult doctors, the administrators who wear too much cologne and ask too many damn questions. You just happen to be the featured attraction."

I groaned. "That doesn't make me feel better."

"No, but it should make you feel less singled out." She took another sip of wine, still smiling. "So why was today strange?"

"I walked into the ICU and two nurses stopped talking mid-conversation. Another one blushed when I asked her a simple question about lab results. And all day, I felt like people were watching me. Like my every move is being reported somewhere."

"You really had no idea people were paying attention to you like that?"

"None whatsoever. I thought I was just...you know. Part of the scenery. Just another doc putting people back together."

"Cole Vaughn." Harper leaned forward, resting her elbows on the table. "You're a six foot two Black man who looks like he's on break from the set of a soapy medical drama. You do not blend in. You're the opposite of blending in. People notice you."

I stared at her for a beat. "You think I look like I belong on TV?"

She didn't blink. "Don't pretend to be modest. You know you're fine as fuck."

My brows shot up. "I do?"

Harper rolled her eyes. "Well, now you're just fishing for compliments."

"Thank you. I'm not, though. I genuinely had no idea anyone was paying attention to me like that."

I picked up my wine glass, and for a moment, it was something to hold onto while I sorted out what she'd just said. "I always figured the safest way to survive in a hospital was to be just visible enough. Keep your head down, do good work, don't invite attention. If you do that, people leave you alone."

"Well, welcome to being objectified. How is it going for you?"

"Not good. I spent all day side-eyeing every person who looked at me. It was exhausting."

"Welcome to being a woman in literally any professional environment."

"It's that bad for you?"

"Being watched?" Harper took a slow sip of her wine. "Oh, yeah. But I figured out a long time ago how to tune it out and do my job. You get used to it after a while."

I shook my head, pulling a face. "I don't want to get used to it. I hate feeling like I'm a bug under a microscope, every move picked apart."

"Then you picked the wrong profession," she said. "Hospitals are fishbowls. Everyone watches everyone. The nurses watch the doctors. The doctors watch the residents and interns. Administration watches all of us, and Legal watches Admin and lord knows who's watching Legal. It's just how it goes."

I realized what she was saying. It was background noise, something you learned to ignore even if you never liked it.

Harper smiled. "In the meantime, you can console yourself with the knowledge that at least the nurses think you're cute."

"That's not consolation, Harper."

Our food arrived at the perfect time. Derek set the plates down, explained each dish in loving detail, asked if we needed anything else. We both said no and he disappeared again.

For a few minutes, there was just the sound of knives and forks, plates being scraped. The short rib was amazing. I barely had to touch it and it just fell apart. I ate slow for once, not like at the hospital where I shoveled something into my mouth between patients.

I glanced up and caught Harper with her eyes closed.

"How did I do picking out a place?" I asked. "Now I'm fishing for compliments."

"Mmmmm. So good." She opened her eyes and smiled at me. "This is delicious. This is my life now."

"Just living at Provisions?"

"Showing up every night, ordering the scallops, dying happy."

Fragments of other conversations reached our table—a couple arguing quietly, a group of friends laughing loudly at the bar, a phone ringing, then quickly silenced. A normal Friday night in a busy restaurant.

Harper's fork clinked on her plate. "Cole...why did you really ask me to dinner?"

I ran my tongue across my teeth, set my fork down, and rested my elbows on the table. "What do you mean?"

"I mean, colleagues having drinks after work, no big deal. A meal out together? That's a big deal, Cole. And not that I have a problem with it, because I'm here. But...what's happening here?"

That was a fair question. I thought about how to answer it and decided on the truth.

"Because I don't talk to many people the way I talk to you. And I wanted to talk more."

Harper went very still.

I continued, pushing the words out before I lost my nerve. "I don't have friends at the hospital. I have colleagues. People I work with, people I respect professionally, people I can stand in an elevator with for thirty seconds without wanting to throw myself down the shaft. But I don't have anyone I actually talk to about real-life shit."

"And you talk to me about real-life shit?"

"Last night was the first real conversation I've had in months. You didn't try to fix anything or offer unsolicited advice or make it about yourself. You listened and responded like we were two people at the same stage of life having a conversation."

Harper's lips curved into a smile. "I'm very good at listening."

"I'm not telling you this to make you feel responsible for my feelings or to put pressure on you," I added. "I'm just explaining why I wanted to see you again. It's not about the investigation. It's not about needing help navigating hospital politics. I like talking to you, and I don't get to do that often."

"Cole—"

"So if that's too much or it makes you uncomfortable, tell me now and we can go back to being colleagues who pass each other in hallways and pretend we don't know each other outside of work."

She didn't answer right away. For a long time, she sat silent, rolling her wine glass in slow, careful circles, the base tracing a ring on the tablecloth. Candlelight glowed off the dark red, catching and shifting as she turned the glass.

Eventually she leaned in, close enough that I could see the light in her eyes, and her voice slipped out soft as a secret. "It's not too much. I like talking to you too."

"Yeah?" I asked, a little breathless, hoping she meant it.

"Yes. You're smart without being condescending the way MDs can be. You're honest without being cruel. And when we talk, you listen." Harper paused, smiling again. "And you make me laugh, which is harder than most people think."

"That's because you have a great sense of humor."

She arched an eyebrow. "Or maybe I'm easily amused."

I smiled and tipped my glass, swallowing the last of the

wine. As if he'd been watching and waiting, Derek refilled both glasses.

"So," Harper said when we were alone again. "If we're both being honest about why we are here..."

"Are we being honest?"

"We're trying to be." The candlelight caught her face; it made her eyes seem darker, almost shadowed. "I've been thinking about last night," she said. "Our conversation."

"And..."

"And what you said—seeing the system clearly, not wasting time on things you can't control—has been replaying in my mind. I don't do...this."

She gestured between us. "I don't go out with colleagues. I went to Rowan's first child's birthday party, but I don't get drinks with Liz Rice or have dinner with Dr. Webb. I keep work at work and my personal life separate."

"Okay. But we are here. Together. So?"

"So talking to you doesn't feel like work."

"What does it feel like?" I asked.

The spread of Harper's smile was a slow, simmering thing. Dangerous. Sultry. I almost forgot we were sitting in the middle of a restaurant.

"I'm still trying to figure that out."

The conversation looped and meandered, touching on everything and nothing. Childhood stories and college mistakes and the worst jobs we had ever had.

Harper told me about working retail during undergrad and having to smile at customers who looked straight through her like she was invisible. I told her about my first day of medical school when I had been so nervous, I dropped a scalpel inside a cadaver and had to fish it out.

"You did not," Harper said, laughing so hard she had to set down her water glass.

"I did. I almost dropped out."

"But you stayed."

I nodded. "Mostly because I didn't know how to tell my dad—well, my step-dad but he's been my dad since he married my mom—that I was punking out. He's a physician, so that was never gonna fly. You never had a day that made you feel like quitting?"

"Oh, of course," Harper admitted. "Especially in the first year. I spent so much time translating, making everyone feel heard, while knowing the organization isn't really going to do anything. I started to wonder if I was part of the problem instead of finding the solution."

"But you stayed."

"Mostly because patients that look like us need to see someone that looks like us in a suit in the admin wing. Some days, I have to wonder," she said, "whether being good at something is reason enough to keep doing it."

"What would you do instead?"

"Live the dream! Buy a plane ticket, disappear for months on end and just exist."

"Nice. Where would you exist?"

"Italy, maybe. Spain. Bali—I don't know, but somewhere where they serve the wine fast and the food slow and people don't apologize for taking three-hour lunches and naps in the middle of the afternoon."

"That sounds incredible."

"What about you?" Harper asked. "If you could do anything other than surgery?"

I thought about it. The wine had made me honest. More honest than I usually was. "Okay, don't laugh, but I'd learn how to cook. *Really* cook, not just throw together chicken and pasta or grill a steak. I want to know how to make food that makes people stop talking and just eat because it's that good."

Harper's expression softened. "That's really specific."

"My mom used to cook like that," I said, nostalgia taking over. "When we were kids, she would spend all day in the kitchen making these elaborate meals. The whole house would smell like whatever she was cooking. We would sit down to eat and nobody would talk for the first few minutes because the food was too good to interrupt with conversation."

"Does she still cook like that?"

"Not often. All the kids grew up and moved out, so most of the time it's just her and my dad. These days, they'd rather go out for a nice meal." I picked at the edge of my napkin. "I keep thinking I should learn how to make those meals she used to make. Kick up my own tradition."

The server appeared with the check. I grabbed the folio before Harper could reach for it.

"I invited you," I said when she opened her mouth to protest.

"Next time is on me, then."

"Next time?"

She smiled. "Next time."

I signed the receipt, left a generous tip because the food had been excellent and the service had been perfectly timed, and stood. I was pleasantly loose, like all my edges had gone soft.

Harper stood, reaching for her coat, and I grabbed it before she could, held it out for her. She gave me a look that was half amused, half surprised, but she let me help her into it.

Outside, the air was cold enough to make my breath visible. Crisp and clean after the warmth of the restaurant.

The parking lot was mostly empty now, just a few scattered cars under the streetlights.

We walked side by side, not talking. My hands were shoved deep in my pockets; hers were wrapped around herself, holding her coat closed against the chill.

At her car, she stopped and turned to face me. "Thank you for inviting me to dinner," she said. "The food was great and the conversation was..." She paused, sighing with a wide smile.

"Same," I said. "Same."

"And for the record..." She stepped closer, enough that I could smell her perfume again. "I'm really glad we ran into each other today."

"Harper," I said in a near-whisper.

"Cole," she replied.

"You think I could kiss you? It's fine if you don't want me to, but I'd really like to."

She pondered the question, pausing for so long I thought she was going to say no. But then...

"Yes."

I closed the distance between us, bringing a hand up to cup her face. Her skin warmed against my palm despite the cool air. Her eyes stayed on mine, dark and intent, until the moment I leaned in, then they fluttered closed.

The kiss began soft. Chaste. My lips against hers, asking the question though I already had the answer. Testing to see if this was real or if I had imagined the electricity between us all night.

She made a small sound in the back of her throat. Stepped even closer, moving her hands up my chest. I deepened the kiss, sliding my other hand around to the small of her back to pull her against me.

Harper opened her mouth; I tasted wine and want and something that felt dangerously close to need.

She kissed the way she did everything else—direct, confident, no hesitation. Her tongue met mine and I forgot about the cold, about the parking lot, about every reason this was complicated.

Her hands slid further north, around my neck. I backed her up against her car, felt her arch into me, heard her breath catch when I gave her a few seconds to breathe.

This was dangerous. This was reckless. This was everything I should not be doing in a public parking lot where anyone could see us.

The sudden vibration against my hip cut through everything. Then the alert—loud, insistent, and impossible to ignore.

"Fuck," I said against her mouth.

"Saved by the bell, I guess," Harper said, her voice breathless.

I finally stepped back, pulled the phone from my pocket, and checked the display. The screen showed:

L1 TRAUMA ALERT ED ETA 8 MIN AH

Level one trauma. Incoming in eight minutes. All hands on deck.

"Damn. I'm on call until midnight."

"Go," she said immediately. "Someone needs you."

"I'm sorry—"

"Cole. This is one instance where you're with someone that understands your job. Go. I'm fine."

She was beautiful. Flushed, lips slightly swollen from kissing, hair messed up from my hands. Beautiful but completely off-limits, and I had just kissed her anyway in a restaurant parking lot like a teenager who couldn't control himself.

"To be continued," I said.

"I know."

I walked to my car, got in, started the engine, and pulled out of the parking lot, heading toward the hospital with her taste still on my lips and the feel of her body burned into my memory like a brand.

This was going to be a problem.

I did not care even a little bit.

Chapter Eight

HARPER

Sunday dinner was a tradition I'd been dodging.

At this point, I'd exhausted every viable excuse and I could practically hear my mother's voice ringing in my ears, daring me to skip out one more time. So I did the only thing I could do—pulled myself together and drove to the sprawling two-story home on Oakmont Drive.

I was the last to show, so I parked at the curb since the driveway was clogged with cars. Aaron's black SUV, Alicia's silver sedan, and Naomi's battered Civic with the political sticker she refused to remove were all jammed in end-to-end.

I grabbed the bottles of wine I'd promised to bring, hip-checking the car door shut behind me. My phone went into my purse, but not before I checked it. Again.

Cole hadn't reached out. I hadn't heard from him since that kiss Friday night, then he had to rush off to the ER.

And that was fine, right? It was a kiss, not a commitment, not a grand gesture, not a promise. We didn't owe each other anything. I was a grown woman with a career and a life, not some teenager waiting by the phone for a boy to call.

Except I'd been keeping an eye on my inbox since Friday night for a message that never came.

Before I could knock, the door swung open and my mother stood there in a flowy caftan, her hair pulled back with a scarf, gold hoops catching the afternoon light.

"There she is!" My mother, Noelle, swept me into one of her hugs that smelled like shea butter and perfume. Her arms were strong around my shoulders, a hug that said 'I love you' and 'where the hell have you been' in equal measure. "We were starting to think you forgot where we live."

"Sorry, Mom. Work's been a lot lately."

She pulled back, hands squeezing my shoulders, brown eyes identical to mine scanning my face. "Mmhmm. Work. Is that all that's keeping you occupied?"

I smirked, catching the hint. "Yes, Mom. Just work."

"Mmmhmmm." She stepped aside, making room for me to pass. "Come on in. The gang's all here."

The house looked the same as it always did, but warmer if possible. Hardwood floors buffed to a shine, family photos from decades past covering every wall, furniture from 2002 that had been reupholstered twice but never replaced because my father said it was in perfectly good condition. Music thumped from a speaker on the back patio, where most of the family was gathered.

Except for my father, who was posted up where he

always was on Sunday afternoons—in his brown leather recliner, feet up, watching a game with the sound muted because my mother didn't allow hootin' and hollerin' in her house on the Lord's Day. He had been retired for more than a decade but still wore the diamond-crusted watch he'd earned for twenty-five years of service with the city's public works department. His hair had faded to white and his waistline was softer now, despite my mother trying to get him to walk around the block with her every evening.

He looked up when I walked in. As always, his face lit up with a bright, wide smile. "Heeey! It's my firstborn baby girl. How you doin'?"

I bent down, pressing my lips against his cheek. "Hey, Daddy. How have you been?"

"Can't complain. I went to the doctor on Thursday. That high blood pressure med my doctor got me on is finally workin'. Your mama's happy about that."

"I'm happy too. That means you'll live forever."

"Not hardly, but since my daughter works at a hospital, I know where I can go when I'm close." He patted my hand, calluses rough against my skin from decades of manual work. "Ain't seen you in a while. You still working too hard?"

I shook my head. "It's almost like I got my work ethic from Byron Sutton."

"A chip off the ole block." He picked up the remote, turned the volume up half a notch when my mother wasn't looking. "Go on out there before them kids come in here looking for you, making all that noise."

Aaron was in the kitchen leaning against the refrigerator, phone in one hand, beer in the other. He worked in IT for a logistics company, and had been divorced for three years from a woman most of us disliked. We were thankful we got to see his daughter, Mia, regularly.

"What's up, A-A-Ron?"

"Sup, Harpy," Aaron said, not even looking up from his phone.

"You look tired. Having a preteen is putting you through it, huh?"

"Mia's fine. It's work that's kicking my ass." He finally glanced up, giving me the once-over. "You do something to your hair?"

"No," I said, suddenly self-conscious.

Mia, who was nine and mostly legs and adolescent attitude, was hunched over her phone at the breakfast bar, thumbs moving across her phone screen. "Aunt Harper!" she squealed, sliding off the bar stool to wrap her arms around my waist. Her face lighting up made my chest tight and my smile wide. "You're here!"

"Of course I'm here." I hugged her, smelling the coconut oil Aaron put in her hair. "You think I'd miss seeing you?"

"You missed two Sundays."

"I know." I pouted. "I'm sorry. Being an adult sucks. How's being a kid lately?"

"It's okay. I got a hundred on my spelling test." She grinned, showing off her braces.

"Okay, genius! Your dad says you have a dance coming up and we're going shopping soon. Do you, uh...have any idea what you want to wear?"

"She does," Aaron butted in, "and she's mad at me because I won't let her buy the tiniest dress in the store. That's why we need you."

"Nooo-uuhhh!" She stomped a foot, her eyes growing

wide. "Aunt Harper, please tell my dad the kids don't wear dresses that go past their knees anymore!"

I held up my hands in mock surrender. "Whoa, I'm Switzerland here. Not taking sides." To cut off the whining I was sure would follow, I made sure to add, "But we'll find something you love and Dad can live with. Deal?"

"Deal!" Mia bounced on her toes, then immediately ran from the room before Aaron could argue.

Alicia came in from the patio, arms open. As she got closer, though, her aim narrowed toward the wine I'd brought. She peered at me over her thick-rimmed glasses as she took the bottles from me.

Alicia could read me better than anyone. That's why I avoided her.

"About time you showed up."

"Hi, Harper. How are you, Harper? Good to see you, Harper."

Alicia rolled her eyes, folding me into a hug. "Hi, Harper. What's...what's going on with you?" she asked, pulling back. "You look different."

I squinted. "I look the same as I always do."

"Mmmm...you definitely look different."

She turned, heading back outside where a large table was in the process of being set for dinner on a closed-in patio. My parents were so proud of their outdoor dining space with heat lamps and a ceiling fan that my father had installed himself.

Naomi was setting the table, mumbling after Alicia yelled at her about how she'd placed the forks. She caught my eye, then abandoned the table to pull me into a hug. Her hair was in long honey blonde goddess locs that fell past her waist, and she wore a vintage Prince t-shirt I was fairly sure she stole from Aaron's closet ages ago.

"You look good," she said, pulling back to study my face. "Like...good."

"I must normally look like I live in a garbage can."

"You're kinda glowing."

"I'm not glowing, Naomi."

"You are glowing." Naomi grinned wider. "Who is he? You can tell me."

"He who? I'm not—"

"Liar."

"Nay, I swear—"

"Your face says you're dating. Fucking, even." She looked past me to Alicia. "She looks dewy and shit. Right?"

Alicia didn't even turn around. "Oh, she's definitely getting dicked down."

Aaron looked up from his phone, beer paused halfway to his mouth. "Wait, what? Harper's dating? Since when?"

"Since never. I'm not dating, and will you three shut up before Mom comes in here? We are in our childhood home."

"This is the most interesting thing that's happened in this family since Aaron's divorce," said Naomi.

"Hey!" Aaron protested.

"It's true." Naomi perched on the edge of the table, clearly settling in. "Okay, so...what's his name? Does he know you're a workaholic who hasn't been on a real date in forever?"

My jaw dropped open. "Excuse you? I date."

"You don't," Naomi said, shaking her head. "You know guys that take you out. You don't have any boo thangs. No boyfriend material. When's the last real romantic date you went on?"

I opened my mouth. Closed it. Tried to remember the

last time I'd gone somewhere with a man that wasn't a convenient conduit to sex.

Well...Friday night. With Cole.

But that wasn't a date. That was dinner. Between colleagues.

Colleagues who'd kissed in a parking lot.

Colleagues who'd kissed like they were trying to breathe each other in.

A colleague I hadn't heard from in two days.

My mother's voice cut through the noise from the doorway. "Alright, everybody. Come and help carry this food to the table so we can eat!"

We gathered around the table with my parents at either end and the rest of us—Alicia and her partner Devon, Aaron and Mia, Naomi, her boyfriend, and me—squeezed in between.

The table was loaded. Pot roast in the center, juice from the slow cooker pooling around tender chunks of beef, carrots, and potatoes. A casserole dish of macaroni and cheese, the top golden and crispy. Cornbread in a cast iron skillet. Sweet tea in a pitcher, already sweating condensation onto the tablecloth.

My father said grace, then the sound of serving spoons hitting plates, forks scraping, and voices overlapping in requests to pass the salt or the butter or the hot sauce that Naomi always drowned her food in filled the room.

This was the rhythm I'd grown up with, the background noise of my childhood. Comfortable and overwhelming at the same time. I felt silly for skipping weeks at a time—these people were annoying, but I loved them. They loved me. And I loved this weekly ritual to reconnect with my siblings, my folks, to narrow my life down to what really mattered.

Most of the time.

"So, Harper." My mother's voice carried across the table, cutting through the chatter. "Anything interesting going on at RMC?"

"Uhm...I mean, always. We're dealing with a complicated case right now."

"You're always dealing with a complicated case." Alicia didn't look up from her plate. "Every time I text you, you're late for a meeting. When was the last time you had a day off?"

"I take days off, Licia. Why are you on my ass today?"

"Language," my mother lobbed gently from the end of the table.

"'Cause I don't want you to die in your office at RMC," Alicia said.

"Harper is ambitious," said Dad, cutting into his pot roast. "Doing big things up at RMC. She's a director—that ain't nothin' to sneeze at. Nothing wrong with it."

"Right," I agreed. "What Daddy said. Nothing wrong with that."

"Sweetheart, you don't have a life outside that hospital," my mother argued. "You're nearly forty and you deserve to have someone special. A partner. Someone who comes home to you at the end of the day."

"I don't disagree, Mom. I just think it'll happen when it's meant to happen."

"You need to help things along. Get a matchmaker. Join a dating site—it's just not natural to be alone." She reached for her tea, ice clinking against the glass. "And don't think I don't know you've been avoiding Sunday dinners because you don't want us asking about your love life."

"And yet, here we are, talking about my love life." I wanted to roll my eyes but didn't want to suffer her wrath. Instead, I filled my mouth with more pot roast.

"I'm not trying to pressure you, baby. I just want you to be happy. And it seems like you spend all your time taking care of other people and none of your time letting anyone take care of you."

I set down my fork with more force than necessary. "Okay, look. I work a lot. I like my job, I'm good at my job, but it's a lot of responsibility and there aren't too many people that look like us in administration at RMC, so I'm trying to stay in the admin wing. We have a case coming up involving a patient death and Diane Hart—y'all know who she is?"

A glance around the table brought nods.

"She's involved. It's the most important file I'll work on all year. I'm focused on this. I'm working. Hard. Am I clear?"

"I still think you're hiding a man from us," Naomi said. "Maybe he's new or—"

"Alright, enough," came a booming voice at the head of the table. My father was not much of a yeller, so when Byron Sutton spoke, everyone listened. "Let's find a different topic of conversation."

"Thank you, Daddy."

My mother picked up her fork. The conversation shifted. Aaron started complaining about his ex-wife's new boyfriend. Mia asked if she could get her hair done in braids for the upcoming dance and lobbied for her and me to shop alone without Aaron.

The normal chaos of a Sutton family dinner returned. But I felt Alicia's eyes on me through the rest of the meal.

Watching. Calculating. Figuring me out the way she always did.

Nosy ass.

After dinner, Alicia cornered me in the kitchen while I was helping put away leftovers.

"I've known you my whole life, you know. You taught me how to ride a bike. You held my hand when I got my period for the first time and thought I was dying."

"This is not kitchen conversation, Alicia."

"My point is I know you. You don't have to tell me anything, but don't bullshit me. You've never been good at that."

My mouth went dry. All the vulnerability, all the restless energy that Cole had stirred in me over the last week surged up and made me want to scream. Instead, I wiped my hands on a towel and spun on her.

"You obviously don't know me well enough to know to back the fuck off."

Before she could respond, my mother swept into the kitchen.

"Harper, you should take some of this roast home," she declared, already reaching for foil. "It's just your dad and me and we won't eat all of this. And I made some greens on Friday, you can take those too. And butter beans; they'll go with the cornbread. Don't forget the macaroni and cheese—"

"Mom, I don't need all that food. Send it home with Aaron," I cut in, but she was already halfway to the fridge.

"Yeah, send it home with me."

"I am sending some home with Aaron, but you'll take some too. Men like a woman with meat on her bones." She pressed a stack of plastic containers to my chest, insisting. "Load up. That wasn't a request."

I left my parents' house with my car loaded down, enough leftovers in the passenger seat to last me at least a week. The drive home was nothing but quiet highway and Mary J. Blige thumping through the speakers.

A check of my phone reported that there was still nothing from Cole.

I had more important things to worry about than a man who could kiss me in a parking lot like that, then disappear into the ether without so much as a "hey, that was fun, let's do that again and more."

By the time I made it home, a mood was coiling through me. Not anger, exactly. Because, if I wanted to, I could text him. I could be a modern woman who didn't wait around, who sent the first message with no worries about rules and norms. Nothing was stopping me from being her.

But I wasn't going to be the one who chased, who put herself out there to be left dangling in the breeze. If he wanted me, he could come get me.

I scooped up my leftovers, headed to the elevator to my apartment, and tried to ignore how ridiculous I felt for letting a man I'd only met last week and kissed exactly once get under my skin like this.

It didn't help that I'd spent the last few days imagining him fucking me senseless, over and over, every time I closed my eyes.

That probably wasn't helping.

* * *

Mondays at Ridgeway Medical Center were always the same, a little parade of things I didn't want to do, emails I didn't want to answer, meetings I definitely didn't want to attend. Since I was in the middle of four distinct cases, my desk was a mess, which was unusual—file folders in a slouching stack, sticky notes migrating off the edge, my tablet wedged somewhere between two compliance manuals.

My coffee had been cold for at least an hour, but I was still drinking it out of stubbornness. I was too lazy to drag myself all the way to the break room to warm it up and I wasn't about to ask Rowan to do it either. They weren't my lackey.

But they could at least pick up on the fact that I needed a refill.

So I was still sipping cold coffee when my internal line rang. The little screen announced Dr. Rice. Figured. She never went through Rowan so they could pretend I'm not available.

"Harper Sutton," I answered, balancing the phone between my ear and shoulder.

"Harper, hi." Her voice came through, brisk as ever. "The Hart family meeting is scheduled for tomorrow. It'll be you and me, Legal, and Dr. Webb."

"Okay. I'll be ready, I guess."

"Good. Two o'clock, twelfth floor conference room." That was all it took for my stomach to take a deep dive. The twelfth floor conference room was reserved for the highest-level, most strictly confidential meetings; using it meant this meeting was a top priority. "I need comprehensive case documentation—timeline, intake, communications, treatment plan, post mortem. The full arsenal. Have it ready by end of day."

"That's a lot to pull together in one day."

"I'm aware. We may not need it all, but we need to be ready. Harper, this is your opportunity to demonstrate we've handled this appropriately."

Which meant this was my chance to make the hospital look good.

"I'll have it ready," I told her. "Should I alert Dr. Vaughn?"

"No," she said, and if it was possible for one syllable to be clipped, that's what it sounded like.

I waited for the explanation I assumed was coming. When none came, I prodded her. "Any reason? You had me interview him and prep him for—"

"Dr. Vaughn will not be attending. We'll handle any clinical queries through the department chair."

"But Dr. Vaughn was the surgeon on call. Excluding him makes it look like we're hiding something."

"We're managing the optics. Keeping the audience small is in our best interest."

"It's really not."

The silence on the other end of the line stretched out so long I thought she'd hung up. "Have the materials ready by end of day," she finally said.

The line went dead before I could respond.

I stared at the phone for a moment, then set it back in its cradle with more force than necessary.

I spent the rest of the day buried in files. When I finally surfaced, the admin wing had gone quiet, everyone else having left at five like normal people.

Rowan knocked on my door frame at six fifteen, looking apologetic. "I pulled everything you requested per your instructions. I'd stay longer, but my partner has class tonight and I'm on kid duty—"

I glanced up from the stack of medical records I'd been cross-referencing with our incident reports. My neck cracked when I turned it.

"Oh, God, Rowan. I am so sorry. I didn't mean for you to stay so late. Please apologize to Nicki for me."

"It's okay. Tomorrow is a big deal. You're here, so I'm

here. And you've been here all day. You didn't even break to eat." They nodded toward the half-sandwich that had grown hard and crusty and the soup that was cold and congealed.

"I'm fine. Promise."

"Mmhmm." They didn't believe me. I didn't believe me either. "Don't stay too late, Harper. Remember, you like to go to war over people."

"Yes. I know. I'm going to finish this, send it off to Dr. Rice, and go home."

"Promise?"

A few minutes and pinky swears to go home in an hour later, Rowan left, pulling my door closed behind them.

They were right. I'd been running on coffee and not much else and it was not doing me any favors.

Over an hour later, I'd finally assembled everything Dr. Rice had asked for. I sent them over, waited for the cursory acknowledgement, then backed everything up and shut down my laptop. I needed to drop off some paperwork in the ER on my way out, so I grabbed the folder from my desk and headed downstairs.

The ER had a mood to it. I felt different when I walked into that department. I wasn't sure I could spend a career in that unit, but some people were clearly born for it.

I weaved between gurneys and staff to reach the unit clerk's station. Behind the counter sat a vaguely familiar woman, her fingers hammering the keyboard at warp speed.

"Help you?" she called.

"Harper Sutton, Risk Management and Patient Advocacy," I said, extending the folder. "Dr. Smith requested this paperwork."

She glanced up just long enough to take it. "I'll see he gets it."

I turned to leave and walked straight into a wall of muscle.

Cole was in rumpled scrubs like he'd been wearing them all day, sleeping in them all night. A stethoscope hung around his neck. His beard was unkempt and his eyes were bloodshot. He seemed tired but alert, like he was running on too little sleep and too much caffeine.

My stomach flipped and flopped at the sight of Cole Vaughn. Relief. Anger. Want. All of it hit me at once and made me dizzy.

"Hey."

Chapter Nine

COLE

I'd been at the hospital all weekend long, save a few hours of actual sleep grabbed in increments between cases. Friday night had ended with a multi-vehicle pileup on the interstate. Three critical patients, all coming in hot. I'd been fighting to keep people alive and hadn't come up for air until Sunday morning.

By then, I felt like an asshole. The kind who kisses a woman, gets her all worked up, then runs off to be a hero and goes radio silent. I was exactly the kind of doctor I'd complained to Harper about at dinner.

I thought about calling her, but I knew I only had one chance to get it right and didn't know what to say aside from, "I'm sorry, I got busy."

That sounded weak.

And right when I was about to dial her number, a gunshot wound came in.

Then a pedestrian versus car. In addition, the flu had decimated the ER staff, so the rest of us were running on fumes. Suddenly it was Monday and I was delirious.

The lounge door opened and Dr. Banks stuck her head in. "Hey. We're getting a couple patients in—Metro is full." I groaned. Metropolitan Community Hospital always claimed they were full and couldn't take more patients, diverting them to RMC. "You here or nah?"

"Nah. I'm burnt to a crisp. I don't even remember where I live anymore."

"A'ight. Go home before someone sees you. I'm here and Pat cut his vacation short. He's about a half hour out."

Thank God. Dr. Pat Mendoza was an angel. If I thought he would stand for it, I'd kiss him.

I could go home. I could sleep for twelve hours straight.

I could call Harper and grovel properly.

"Yeah. That sounds like a great idea." I pushed myself up off the lumpy lounge couch, every joint protesting. I wasn't in my twenties anymore. Hell, I wasn't in my thirties anymore. I couldn't do too many of these marathon weekends.

I grabbed my jacket from my locker and headed toward the exit, winding through the ER because it was faster. I was halfway to the door when I saw Harper.

Barreling toward me, her face in her phone, clearly heading home for the night.

She was...beautiful. Even exhausted, even annoyed—I could tell from twenty feet away—she was beautiful.

I wasn't sure if she saw me and was pretending not to or if she hadn't seen me, but I planted myself in her way and waited for the collision.

When she ran into me, she jumped back in surprise. There was shock...then I watched her force her expression back to nonchalance.

"Harper...hey."

"Dr. Vaughn." Her tone was cold. I was in trouble and deserved to be.

"Uh, I'm glad I ran into you. Or you ran into me. You got a minute to catch up?"

"It's been a long day, Dr. Vaughn. I'm on my way out. We can talk in the morning—"

"Harper. It'll only take a minute. Please."

I watched her consider it, weigh whether I was worth the effort. The *please* probably helped—I heard how my voice went soft on that word.

"Fine. What?"

I looked around. The ER was too crowded. Too many eyes, too many ears. And a nosy group chat.

"Not here. Let's go this way."

I led her down the corridor past radiology, past the lab, into a section of the hospital that was quieter this time of night. I stopped in front of a supply closet I knew would be unlocked and pulled her in, locking the door behind us.

The space was small with narrow shelves lining the walls and a small table pushed against one wall. There was barely room for two people to stand without touching.

"Harper, listen, I'm—"

"You didn't text me." Her words hit with such force, it felt like she'd punched me in the face. "We had all that meaningful conversation about how you *love* talking to me, then you shoved your tongue down my throat, then you ran off...and I don't even rate a hello the next morning? It's just...crickets? All weekend?"

"I know. That's why I wanted to talk. I'm so, so—"

"It's been days, Cole. What was that about? It would have been better if we'd just not gone there. I don't have any openings on the cut-buddy calendar."

"Okay, I didn't *disappear*, Harper. You said you understood a surgeon's life. I got pulled into a case that turned into a nightmare and it's been hell ever since. You work here —you couldn't check to see how busy the ER was over the weekend? I've been fighting for my damn life down here. I could barely remember my own name, much less form a coherent sentence."

I watched her try hard to maintain her pout, but it was quickly disappearing. I was wrong for not at least texting her...but I had warned her about what my life was like.

As expected, her shoulders dropped a fraction. "You could have given me a heads-up at least."

"I could have. I should have. I realized how long it had been and I felt terrible. I decided I'd talk to you in person today, apologize properly. Just...the day got away from me, and..."

I shrugged my shoulders, hoping I looked as pathetic as I felt. "I'm sorry."

Harper studied my face in the dim overhead light, her eyes drifting from the bags under my eyes to the stubble shadowing my jaw, to the scrubs I'd been wearing for God knows how long.

"Well, you do look terrible," she said.

"Thanks. That's what every man wants to hear from a woman he's into."

"So..." She crossed her arms over her chest, which pushed her breasts up in a way that was distracting under the circumstances. "Apologize, then."

I moved in, propping an arm on a shelf above her head.

This close, I could see the deep brown of her eyes and watched the way her pupils dilated slightly.

"So...I know we work together. I know it's a complicated situation. But I won't pretend that kiss on Friday night didn't happen. I won't pretend I've stopped thinking about you and won't pretend I don't want it to happen again. I'm sorry," I said, dropping my tone low. "I'm sorry I didn't text. I'm sorry I made you think I was blowing you off. I'm sorry I—"

She kissed me.

Put that beautiful mouth right on me. I was surprised, but only because I'd been prepared to grovel more. The shock of it knocked a grunt from my throat before I could catch myself. I cupped her face, cradling her jaw in my palms, and kissed her back like I'd been starving for it, my tongue sweeping into her mouth.

Her lips were soft and she opened for me immediately, her tongue slick and warm as it slid against mine, the friction of it making my knees weak. She moaned, pressing herself up against me. The feel and the sound went straight south.

"I missed you," I whispered against her mouth. "I haven't stopped thinking about you. About doing more than kissing you. I really...*really* want to do more than kiss you."

"Prove it."

My hands slid down to her waist, gripping her hips. "Prove I missed you? That I haven't stopped thinking about you?"

"The more than kissing me part. That."

My brain short-circuited. Blood rushed through my body so fast I felt dizzy.

But I wasn't about to decline.

I gripped her waist and lifted her onto the table in one

smooth motion, stepping between her legs. My hands slid under her skirt, up her thighs. Her skin was so warm, so soft under my palms.

"Like here? In this closet?"

She shrugged, offering a grin with a brief look around the space. "You have a better idea?"

I did not. I kissed her again, slower, deeper, savoring her lips. One hand tangled in her hair while the other worked at the buttons of her blouse. When I got it open, I let my palm slide inside.

Beneath my fingertips, her bra felt expensive—smooth satin with delicate lace. Through the fabric, I found her nipple already hardening at my touch. I flicked it gently and Harper's head fell back against the shelf behind her with a soft thud, her breath coming out in a shaky exhale.

"God, Cole..."

I leaned in to kiss the column of her throat, tasting the salt of her skin. "Harper...if we're singing the same song, this is a bad idea."

"I know. I don't care right now."

"Someone could walk in."

"You locked the door," she said.

"Harper—"

"Cole, please." The words were ragged at the edges, a plea that went straight to my nerve center. "If you don't fuck me right now in this closet, I'm going to lose my mind."

Whatever control I had left snapped like a rubber band. My hands moved faster, pulling her blouse open the rest of the way. I bent my head to her breast, taking her nipple into my mouth through the lace, sucking hard enough to make her arch against me.

I reached under her skirt, my fingers tracing up her inner thigh. The heat radiating from her was obscene before

I even touched her. When I found the edge of her panties, the fabric was already soaked through. I pressed my thumb against her damp center and felt her pulse against me, her hips rising in response.

"You're so wet, baby. Is that for me?"

"I've been thinking about doing more than kissing you all weekend too."

A low, primal groan rolled from my lips. I pushed her panties to the side, slipping two fingers through her lips. Her clit was swollen, yearning for attention. I barely brushed a fingertip over her before Harper gasped, then clamped a hand around the back of my neck. Her nails dug into my skin as she pulled my mouth back to hers.

She kissed me as I circled her clit, painfully slow at first, then gradually increasing the pressure.

"More," she pleaded against my lips. "Please, Cole, I need more."

I worked her slow, watching her face. Cataloging every reaction— how her breath hitched when I pressed just right, the sultry roll of her hips against my hand when I didn't give her enough pressure, how she dug her heels into the wall behind me, using the leverage to grind hard against my fingers.

She was shameless. Desperate. Sexy.

I pushed one finger inside her, then two, feeling her pulse around me. She was more than ready, slick and hot. I could barely think straight, my need for her becoming a living thing, turning my blood molten. My scrubs offered nothing to disguise the way my body strained for her, every inch of me aching to bury myself inside her that second.

I pulled my fingers from her and brought them to my mouth, licking her from my skin while she watched, heat smoldering in her eyes. I let her see how much I liked it, how much I wanted her.

"You taste so good to me."

Harper's eyes fluttered closed at that, her lips parting as she let out a shaky breath. When she opened them again, the look she gave me was pure fire.

"Stop talking and fuck me, Cole."

"Hey, hey, hey, bossy. I know you're used to being in control, but relax." I shoved my scrub pants down along with my boxers. "You're not leaving this room until I take care of you."

Her eyes went dark as she wriggled out of her panties and flicked them over my shoulder. My dick strained, heavy and aching, the tip already slick. She wrapped her fingers around me, slow at first, then stroked once. Twice. The sensation almost undid me right there.

"Payback, huh?" I rumbled, closing my eyes.

"So...I'm on birth control," she said suddenly. "And I stay current on tests. I can send you my recent results."

"Good," I said, trying to return to earth. "Uhm, I tested a few months ago when I had my physical, and I haven't been active."

I paused, glancing down at her hand still wrapped around me. "I really need to be inside you, Harper. Right now. We good?"

"Oh." She laughed and reluctantly let go. "Yeah. We're good."

I drew in a ragged breath, my hands gripping her thighs. Every muscle in my body vibrated with anticipation. I felt her pulse through her skin and I was so hard it almost hurt.

Our eyes locked, and I saw something there that went deeper than lust. I didn't want to lose myself in her just because I could; I wanted this to be something she wanted too. More than a passing impulse, more than a desperate fuck in a closet.

Even if that was exactly what it was.

"Harper. You're sure?"

She stared at me, incredulous, as if I'd just asked her whether the sky was blue. She arched her back a little, her thighs locking tight around my hips.

"Cole. Stop being a gentleman and fu—"

That was all I needed to hear.

I angled my hips forward, sinking into her in a slow, deliberate stroke. The sensation hit me like a freight train—she was so tight, so warm, so wet that for a moment, I couldn't breathe. My vision blurred at the edges and I had to brace myself to keep from collapsing.

"Goddamn, Harper," I growled into her ear. I suppressed a moan at the sensation of being completely surrounded by her.

She felt good. Better than good. Better than anything I'd felt in years. Maybe ever.

I started slow, pulling almost all the way out before sliding back in, savoring every second of being inside her. Harper met my rhythm, matching me thrust for thrust.

"Harder. Fuck me hard," she managed.

I obliged, setting a rhythm that had her panting, each thrust deeper than the last. The table creaked beneath us, supplies rattling on the shelves.

"You are doing. The. Damn. Thing. Cole. Shit!" She sat up and bit my shoulder hard enough to make me hiss. "Don't stop. Make me come."

"Like that?" I asked against her neck. "It's good to you?"

She nodded, her breath coming in short bursts. "So good. God, so fucking good."

I fucked her in that storage closet.

I fucked her in strong, powerful strokes, every thrust driving her up the table a fraction of an inch, every retreat pulling a raw sound from her throat.

I fucked her with a juicy thigh in each hand, pulling her to me like it was what I was born to do. Every time I bottomed out, she made this whimpering sound that made my dick pulse.

I already didn't know how I could go the rest of my life not hearing that again and again and again.

I was losing it. My rhythm faltered, hips pumping with an urgency I found it hard to control. I was close. Too close.

"I am gonna fucking come in this beautiful pussy," I growled. "But I want you to get yours first. Whatever you gotta do to get there, you do it."

Harper's eyes flashed bright and grew wide. One of her hands slipped between us, her fingers finding her clit while I continued to thrust into her. The sight of her touching herself while I was buried deep almost took me over the edge.

"Yeah, I like that," I breathed, watching her face contort. I felt her pulsing around me. "Your pussy's talking to me. Let me see you come."

Harper's breathing quickened. She bit her lip, eyes squeezed shut, then, "Fuck! Cole!" she whispered, breathless and desperate. "Oh my God, I'm...I'm coming! I'm coming!"

Her whole body convulsed beneath me, every muscle taut to a breaking point. Her mouth dropped open and she bit back a scream. Her pussy clamped down on my dick with a force I'd never felt before, so tight and greedy it set off a chain reaction deep in my gut.

Her legs trembled, kicking helplessly, her hands behind my neck as she pulled me to her, locking her mouth against mine. The sound of her orgasm, her cries muffled, pushed me over the edge. My hips jerked forward one final time and I buried myself deep, my release hitting like a sledgehammer. I groaned, my body shaking as I emptied myself inside her.

We stayed joined until after the aftershocks pulsed around me. Both of us breathing hard, our foreheads pressed together, half-dressed and slick with sweat.

"Well, damn, Ms. Sutton." I lifted my head, half a smile on my lips.

"Do not start," she said, almost laughing.

"I just wish I knew a supply closet was so hot."

She giggled. "Right? Let me find out this is our spot."

"Say less. Mondays at seven can be the witching hour."

"I mean, I'm hoping we see a bed at some point."

"You right. You right. But uhm, that was..."

"Necessary," she finished. She looked sated. "I don't know about you, but I needed that."

I laughed, breathless and genuine. "Yeah. Same."

I pulled out carefully and Harper hopped down from the table. We cleaned up quickly with paper towels we found in a box on the shelves in an attempt to look less freshly fucked.

Harper tried to adjust her skirt while I helped button her blouse. Well, I tried.

"You're a trauma surgeon but you can't get the little button in the little hole?" she teased.

"I'm exhausted and I just had amazing sex in a supply closet at work. Forgive me if I'm not on my A game right now."

"This was a wild idea."

"Completely." I grinned. "When can we do it again?"

She laughed. "Sheesh. Insatiable, much?"

"That was the best sex I've had in years."

"It was pretty good."

"Pretty good?" My eyebrows shot up. "Harper...we almost broke that table."

She clicked her tongue. "Your ego is showing, Dr. Vaughn."

"Whatever. I almost made you cry." I kissed her, soft and lingering, my hand gentle on the back of her neck. "I really am sorry I didn't text you. I hope I made it up to you."

"You did. I had no plans to chase you, but the phone does work both ways."

"I'd like for us to both do better. Any chance you want to come home with me tonight?"

"I'm tempted," she said, looking a little sad. "I really am. Thing is...I'm not supposed to tell you this, but the meeting with the Hart family is tomorrow. I want to look everything over one more time."

Reality crashed back in. The investigation. Diane Hart. The fact that I was potentially about to lose my career.

And I'd just fucked the woman who was supposed to be facilitating the review. In a supply closet. At work.

"Tomorrow?" I repeated.

"Dr. Rice called me this morning. I spent today prepping."

"Okay. They don't want me there?"

"No," she replied with a sigh. I knew what it meant. "They're keeping you out of it. For now."

"I wish I thought that was a good thing." I pushed out a hard breath. "Thanks for the heads-up."

"I'll keep you posted on how it goes."

"Okay." I hesitated, then decided to go for it. "Harper, we...this—"

"I know. We shouldn't have, but we did already, so..."

Harper shrugged her shoulders. "For now, let's just enjoy the afterglow."

She unlocked the door, checked the hallway, then slipped out. I waited ten seconds before I followed her.

"Hey," I whispered.

She turned. I was still standing in the doorway of the supply closet, looking as wrecked as I felt.

"For the record," I said, keeping my voice low, "that case is the last thing I'll be thinking about tonight."

She beamed a smile at me. "Good. I'd prefer it if I were dominating your attention. I'll text you after I finish prepping. I may have further thoughts to share."

I watched her walk away, tracking the bounce of her ass cheeks under her skirt. Then I remembered...

I went back to the closet, found her panties, and shoved them in my pocket.

I forced myself to check on a few patients, then bullshit with Banks for twenty minutes before leaving the hospital. That wasn't the smartest thing I'd ever done. It was, quite honestly, the definition of reckless.

That was why I'd enjoyed it so much.

As soon as I got in the car, my phone buzzed with her name lighting up the screen.

HARPER:

Just pulled in at home. I feel great.

ME:

Me too. By the way, I picked up your panties. Very nice.

There was a pause that I read as breathless.

HARPER:

Shit. I was halfway home when I realized. I'll get them back from you.

I retrieved them from my pocket and held them up, running the fabric between my fingers.

ME:

Nah, you're not getting these back. I rescued them. They're mine.

HARPER:

You can't keep my underwear, Cole.

ME:

Come get 'em

HARPER:

In time, Dr. Vaughn

ME:

We are gonna sleep good tonight.

HARPER:

Eventually.

I frowned at my phone.

ME:

What do you mean, eventually? You got plans? You got ENERGY for plans?

HARPER:

My plans are to pour a glass of wine and pull out my vibrator while I imagine us in that closet and give myself an encore.

I sat in my parking spot staring at my phone, already stirring back to life.

ME:

Oh.

I think I'm jealous.

HARPER:

Well, if you want me to wait until you can join in the fun, FaceTime me when you're ready. I'll give you something you can do with my panties.

My brain shorted out at the mental image of her on my screen, legs parted, fingers stroking...

The last of my self-control was fried.

ME:

Oh, word? I'm on my way home. Don't start without me.

Chapter Ten

HARPER

The twelfth floor conference room was an impressive space, meant to frighten and amaze in the same breath. Floor-to-ceiling windows overlooked the city with a view of the river curling through downtown. The carpet was expensive and high-end art hung along the walls. A long walnut table dominated the room, Italian leather chairs ringing it.

The room radiated power.

I arrived early, toting my tablet, leather portfolio, and binder full of notes. Dr. Rice was already there, seated at the head of the table, scrolling her phone.

She glanced up, then checked her watch. "Perfect timing. Take the far end by the projector. I'll handle the introductions, then you'll walk through your findings. We'll field their questions after."

No pleasantries. Just orders issued in that fake professional tone.

I walked to the far end and set my things down. After connecting my tablet to the display, I took my seat and tried to ignore the nervous flutter in my stomach.

Two attorneys from Morrison & Chase, the hospital's legal counsel, arrived next, taking their seats at the table—Adrienne Westfield and Gerald Clark. The rumor mill said they billed nearly a thousand dollars an hour. They looked like they billed a thousand dollars an hour.

Dr. Webb entered, choosing a seat next to me. He was a great department chair, but an even better politician. He knew how to read a room, how to protect his interests. Or himself.

"Morning, Harper," he said.

I nodded as everyone settled into an uneasy quiet.

Then the door opened again.

Diane Hart entered the room, and though we'd never met, I knew her immediately. A petite woman in her mid-fifties with a salt-and-pepper short natural cut, she maintained a mask of composure that couldn't hide what her body revealed—eyes puffy and red-rimmed, shoulders slumped, hands pale as they clutched her bag. This was a woman who'd lost someone she loved, who was looking for answers.

Or she was looking for someone to blame.

My job, as I saw it, was to give her some peace. And to make sure she didn't find those answers at Cole's expense.

Behind Diane came Rachel Gaines, in a designer suit with a Hermès briefcase. I'd done my homework. Rachel specialized in medical malpractice with a formidable track record. Seventy-three percent settlement rate, with the remaining cases going to trial where she'd won more often than not. She was ruthless and expensive. She didn't take cases she couldn't win.

The fact that she was here meant she saw an opening.

"Good afternoon," she said, her voice pitched to carry without being loud. "I'm Rachel Gaines, attorney for the Hart family."

Introductions went around the table. When Rachel got to me, her handshake was firm, her piercing blue eyes giving me a quick assessment.

"Harper Sutton is our Director of Risk Management and Patient Advocacy," said Dr. Rice. "She'll be presenting the majority of the material today."

"Ms. Sutton," Rachel replied. "I've heard good things about your work."

I doubted that was true, but I smiled anyway. "Thank you."

Rachel guided Diane to a chair, then took the seat beside her. She pulled a legal pad and pen from her briefcase, then folded her hands and glanced at Dr. Rice.

The room felt smaller, the air thicker. My pulse thrummed in my ears.

Dr. Rice began. "We want to first express our deep sympathies to you and your family, Mrs. Hart. I can't begin to imagine how hard this has been for you." She didn't even glance at Diane as she said it. "We're committed to transparency as we work through the facts in this case, and we welcome any questions you may have today."

She hit all the right notes without committing to anything. Or admitting anything.

Rachel listened with a neutral expression, her pen tapping against her legal pad. Diane stared at the table, jaw working like she was trying not to cry.

"Ms. Sutton has prepared a comprehensive review of

Mr. Greene's care," Dr. Rice continued. "Harper, would you walk us through your findings?"

I stood, picked up the remote, and moved to a position where I could see both the screen and the table. "Thank you, Dr. Rice."

I looked at Diane first, making eye contact.

"Mrs. Hart, losing someone you love is never easy, and I know the circumstances of your grandfather's death have raised questions for you and your family. I've spent the past several days reviewing every aspect of Mr. Greene's care. I'd like to walk you through that timeline and answer any questions you have."

I clicked to my first slide. "Mr. Greene arrived at the ER at 1:17 PM, unresponsive with dangerously low blood pressure and a distended abdomen. An ultrasound revealed a ruptured aortic aneurysm—essentially a burst in the main artery carrying blood through the abdomen. This is a life-threatening emergency with a ninety percent mortality rate. The trauma team made the decision to transfer him immediately to surgery."

I advanced to the next slide.

"At 1:52 PM, our staff reached out to you regarding Mr. Greene's care. We left word to please call back at your earliest convenience."

Rachel stopped tapping her pen.

"Surgery began at 2:11 PM. Despite aggressive resuscitation, transfusions, and attempts to repair the rupture, Mr. Greene's condition continued to deteriorate. He went into cardiac arrest at 2:27 PM. Dr. Vaughn called time of death."

I let the silence settle, then clicked forward to my final slide.

"Mrs. Hart, I know this detail doesn't make the loss any

easier. However, I can assure you that your grandfather received appropriate, aggressive care from a highly skilled team. Every decision was consistent with standard trauma protocols. The outcome was tragic, but it wasn't due to failure to care for him."

Diane's face crumpled. She pressed a hand to her mouth, shoulders shaking with silent sobs. Rachel placed a hand on her arm—a gesture that was both comforting and possessive. Then she looked at me.

"Ms. Sutton, that was very thorough. Thank you."

"Of course."

"I do have some questions."

I'd been expecting that. I nodded, kept my expression open. "Please."

Rachel flipped back through her notes, not appearing to be in any hurry. I seethed. I despised this courtroom trick, designed to transfer dominance and control of the room to her.

"What exactly did the message from RMC Emergency Room to Mrs. Hart say?"

I pulled up the documentation. "The nurse identified herself, said she was calling from Ridgeway Medical Center ER, and asked her to call back."

"The nurse didn't note the severity of Mr. Greene's condition. She didn't use the words 'life-threatening emergency.' Not 'your grandfather is dying.' Just...call back?"

"You know as well as I do that there's only so much we can convey in a voicemail message due to privacy laws—"

"The message didn't convey severity within privacy laws," Rachel said. "Mr. Greene was in the sunset of his life with several comorbidities, and Brookside often called an ambulance for the slightest inconvenience. It was not unusual for Mrs. Hart to receive a call about her grandfather being seen. So there was nothing in the message that translated to the need to rush to the hospital."

I measured my words carefully. "Our priority is stabilizing the patient and notifying next of kin. We follow established protocols to ensure the standard of care is the same across—"

"How many attempts were made to reach Mrs. Hart before surgery?" Rachel asked.

I checked my notes, though I knew this case by heart. "We placed a call six minutes before Mr. Greene was transferred to the OR."

"One call. One voicemail. Six minutes." Rachel looked around the table. "That's reasonable effort? That's established protocol?"

"In emergency situations," Gerald said, "informed consent is implied when a patient is unable to consent and family is unavailable. The phone call is a courtesy."

"The one phone call that doesn't convey severity? If this were your grandfather three hours away, would you understand 'call us at the hospital' to mean he was actively dying?"

"I can't understand any situation where a call from the hospital doesn't indicate urgency," I argued. "The priority is saving the patient's life."

"If the outcome was almost certainly fatal, the family had a right to decide whether their loved one should die in an operating room or with dignity."

A choked sob poured from Diane, soft but devastating.

"Our protocols require documentation of family notification," said Dr. Rice. "That documentation exists."

"Your protocols don't require that the family actually be reached or be given enough information to make an informed decision," Rachel argued. "Mrs. Hart learned her grandfather had died via a cold, impersonal phone call. She didn't get to say goodbye. She didn't get to hold his hand. She didn't even get to make the decision about whether surgery was what he would have wanted. Because no one gave her the option to rush to the hospital."

Rachel let the moment sit. Then she looked at me.

"Who made the decision to proceed with surgery without next of kin authorization?"

"Dr. Cole Vaughn, the on-call trauma surgeon."

"And Dr. Vaughn made that decision without speaking to anyone in administration? Literally no one backing him up?"

"Our surgeons are in life-and-death situations all day," Dr. Webb argued. "He made his decision based on Mr. Greene's presentation, prognosis, and emergency protocols."

"So this wasn't a hospital decision," Rachel said. "This was one person unilaterally choosing to proceed."

I felt the trap closing. "Dr. Vaughn consulted with the attending and surgical team."

"But ultimately, Dr. Vaughn decided," Rachel pressed.

"Dr. Vaughn is an excellent trauma surgeon with an impeccable record," said Dr. Webb. "His decision-making in this situation was sound."

"I'm sure it was," Rachel said, drawing her hands back. "So, we'd like to hear from Dr. Vaughn."

My stomach dropped. "I—I'm sorry?"

"Mrs. Hart deserves to hear directly from the surgeon that treated him. She deserves to look him in the eye and ask why her grandfather died alone."

"Ms. Gaines—" I started.

"This isn't about blame," Rachel said, her hands up in surrender. "This is about understanding. Mrs. Hart has questions only Dr. Vaughn can answer. Surely Ridgeway has nothing to hide. Unless there's a reason you don't want him in this room."

It was a perfect trap. We looked guilty if we refused.

"Of course," Dr. Rice said. "I'm sure Dr. Vaughn would be happy to—"

"No!" I said, nearly shouted. Every head in the room turned toward me.

Dr. Rice's eyes narrowed slightly—a warning I chose to ignore.

"Dr. Vaughn's surgical notes are comprehensive. Asking him to sit in this room and defend real-time medical decisions to a grieving family is inappropriate. It's not fair to him, and frankly, it's not fair to Mrs. Hart."

Rachel's eyebrow arched. "You don't think Mrs. Hart deserves to speak with her grandfather's surgeon?"

"I think Mrs. Hart deserves accurate, complete information about her grandfather's care," I said. "Which I've provided. Putting Dr. Vaughn in this room where his medical judgment will be second-guessed by people who weren't there is inappropriate."

"Harper," Dr. Rice said quietly. It was a warning.

I ignored her, my eyes trained on Rachel.

"If you have specific clinical questions, I can arrange for written responses. I can set up a separate meeting with medical experts to review the operative report. But bringing him into a meeting like this, where he'll be expected to justify how he tried to save someone's life? That reeks of building a case for negligence where none exists."

Rachel smiled, but it wasn't pleasant. "Ms. Sutton, I appreciate your vigorous defense of Dr. Vaughn, but I have to wonder why you're so resistant. If Dr. Vaughn's care was appropriate, then he should have no problem explaining it to Mrs. Hart. Unless there's something about those decisions that you think won't stand up to scrutiny?"

"That's not what I'm saying—"

"Because from where I'm sitting, it looks like you're trying hard to keep Dr. Vaughn away from my client. And that makes me wonder what you're trying to hide."

Adrienne cleared her throat. "Ms. Gaines, we can arrange for Dr. Vaughn to attend a follow-up meeting."

Webb nodded. "Dr. Vaughn is capable of explaining his decisions."

Rachel pulled out her phone. "How's next Tuesday? That should give Dr. Vaughn time to prepare."

Time to prepare for his own execution.

Dr. Rice confirmed. "We'll have Dr. Vaughn ready to discuss his findings."

"Perfect." Rachel looked at Diane, who was still staring at the table, tears streaming silently. "Mrs. Hart, let's get you home."

Diane stood slowly, mechanically. She picked up her purse, clutched it to her chest, and finally looked up at me. Her eyes were devastated.

"I just want to understand," she said, her voice barely above a whisper.

The words hit me like a physical blow.

"Mrs. Hart," I said gently. "I know this is hard. I know you're looking for answers. But I promise you, your grandfather received excellent care. Dr. Vaughn did everything he could."

"Then he should be able to tell me that himself," Diane said.

Rachel squeezed her shoulder. "He will, Mrs. Hart. Next week, you'll hear directly from him."

Then she and Diane left, the door closing behind them with a soft click that somehow felt louder than a slam.

The room exhaled. Gerald and Adrienne immediately began strategizing. Dr. Webb looked at his watch, muttered something about needing to get to other meetings, and stood to leave.

I started packing up my things, hands moving mechanically while my mind raced.

I'd just watched them set Cole up. Watched them turn him from a skilled surgeon who'd made the right call into a lone actor whose judgment would be questioned, whose career could be sacrificed to appease a donor family.

And I'd stood there and let it happen.

"Harper."

I looked up. Gerald and Adrienne were gathering their things.

"That was good work," Gerald said. "Thorough presentation."

"Until the end," Adrienne added. "Next time, let us handle the objections. That's what we're here for."

"I didn't see or hear either of you actually doing that," I said. "It would be great if you could both find your voices by next week. Dr. Vaughn will need you."

When they left, it was just me and Dr. Rice.

"What the hell was that?" I asked before she could start.

Dr. Rice's eyebrow arched slightly. "Excuse me?"

I tossed my binder back down to the table. "You kept Cole out of this meeting so you could frame this as his decision, not hospital policy. You let Rachel Gaines build her case that this was about one surgeon's judgment, not RMC protocols. And now you're feeding him to the Hart family."

"I'm doing what's best for RMC," Dr. Rice said.

"You're throwing a good surgeon under the bus to protect donor relationships."

Dr. Rice walked to the window, her arms crossed. "Harper, let's be very clear about something. Diane Hart's family has contributed over fifteen million dollars to this hospital over the past decade. Her husband sits on two foundation boards. The Board chairman plays golf with Richard Hart every Sunday. Do you understand what that means?"

"You'll sacrifice Cole's career to keep them happy."

"It means," Dr. Rice said, her tone dropping to something harder, colder, "that we cannot afford to be on the wrong side of this family. It means that fifteen million dollars is a conservative estimate of what the Hart family could redirect to other hospitals. The Board chairman has already called me twice about this case. We are under a microscope, and the only way to make this go away is to give them what they want."

"Which is Cole's head on a platter?"

"Which is answers," Dr. Rice corrected. "If Cole's care was appropriate, then he has nothing to worry about. He'll sit in that meeting, answer questions, and they'll see everything was done correctly."

"You don't believe that." I stared at her. "You know exactly what's going to happen—Rachel Gaines is going to paint Cole as a cowboy who prioritized his own judgment over family input. And you're going to let them make Cole the villain because it's easier than admitting that sometimes people die and it's nobody's fault."

"That's not what's happening here."

"That's exactly what's happening here," I shot back. "You're isolating him so that if this goes to litigation, the hospital can claim he acted independently."

Dr. Rice's expression didn't change. "What I believe,"

she said slowly, "is that this hospital will not take responsibility for an outcome that was essentially a Hail Mary. Cole knew it when he made the call."

She moved closer, sounding more menacing by the second. "If the family needs someone to hold accountable, then Cole needs to be prepared to defend it."

"He made the right call."

"Then he'll be fine," Dr. Rice said, like it was that simple.

"Liz—"

"No." Her tone was cold and hard as a rock. "You don't get to 'Liz' me right now, Ms. Sutton. You undermined me, openly disagreed with the direction I set in front of outside counsel, in front of Dr. Webb, in front of the hospital's legal team. Do you have any idea how that looks?"

"I was protecting RMC—"

"You were protecting Dr. Vaughn," she interrupted. "Which is not your job. Your job is to manage risk. Not to be Dr. Vaughn's personal advocate."

My jaw clenched. "My job includes protecting our staff from being railroaded."

"Your job is whatever I say it is." Dr. Rice moved back to the table, leaning forward. "And right now, I'm saying that we need to handle this situation carefully, strategically, and with the hospital's best interests as the priority. Not Cole Vaughn's feelings."

"Cole's career is part of this hospital's interests. He's an excellent surgeon with a spotless record. If you let them destroy that—"

"No one is getting destroyed, Harper! But we will not wring our hands about one surgeon at the expense of the entire institution. Do you understand what I'm saying?"

I understood perfectly. If someone had to burn, it

wouldn't be Ridgeway Medical Center. It would be Cole Vaughn.

"This is wrong."

"This is reality. If you can't accept that, then you're not the right person for this role."

The threat landed like a slap.

"Are you firing me?" I asked.

"Are you going to do your job? Can you put the hospital first? Can you manage this case objectively, without letting personal feelings about Dr. Vaughn cloud your judgment?"

Personal feelings.

The phrase lingered between us like smoke. My pulse quickened as I wondered if she was implying what I thought she was—if rumors had reached her.

I straightened my spine. "My assessment of Dr. Vaughn's decision-making is based on medical protocols and the facts of the case, nothing more."

"Then prove it," Dr. Rice said. "I want you to prepare him. Make sure he understands what's at stake. Make sure he knows how to present himself—calm, professional, empathetic. Make sure he doesn't walk into the room defensive or combative."

She paused for effect, then added, "In other words, make sure he doesn't fuck this up, because the hospital is not prepared to stand behind him if his stance veers off script. Am I clear?"

I could tell her to go to hell. I could quit on the spot.

But I thought about my salary, the benefits, the promotion I'd spent years crawling toward. I thought about my luxury apartment and my late model vehicle and how getting fired from a director-level position would look on a résumé.

I thought about everything I'd built, brick by brick. It

would take nothing for someone in Dr. Rice's position to knock it all down.

And I hated myself a little for not being brave enough to walk away.

Dr. Rice gathered her things, her attention already shifting to the next meeting. "I want a full prep session with Dr. Vaughn by Monday afternoon. Send me your notes afterward."

"Fine."

"And Harper?" She looked up. "I meant what I said. I need to know you can handle this objectively. If I think for one second that you're compromising this hospital's interests because of some personal loyalty to Dr. Vaughn, we're going to have a much more serious conversation. Am I being understood?"

"Yes," I replied, seething that I had to agree. She roped me into this case because Mrs. Hart and Dr. Vaughn were Black, and for no other reason. She thought I'd smile and play the good employee and gently guide Cole through RMC fucking him over.

She opened the door and stomped out of my office. I was right behind her a few moments later. I had to get out of the building.

Right now.

I rode the elevator down in silence, staring at my reflection in the stainless steel. I prayed I'd be able to get to my car without anyone seeing the little earthquakes under my skin.

The employee parking garage was humid. I unlocked my car, slid into the driver's seat, and sat there with both hands on the wheel.

Everything Dr. Rice said kept circling in my mind. The threat, not even veiled, was a blunt blade pressed to my spine. How quick she was to toss Cole's life onto the scale to steady the hospital's standing with a donor family worth fifteen million.

And I let her. I let myself get swept along, too busy protecting my own skin to do the right thing.

I pulled out my phone, scrolled, and dialed.

Cole picked up on the second ring. "Hey."

Just hearing his voice did something to me, calmed my nerves in a way I hadn't expected. I didn't know this man well enough to be comforted by the sound of his voice.

"Hi. Are you busy?"

"Uhm, nah. I took today off since I worked all weekend. Are you trying to download about the meeting? Webb called a bit ago."

"Yeah. Actually, I need to see you. Can we meet up somewhere?"

"I figured you might reach out." His voice dropped, concerned. "I'm at home. You want to come through? I'll text you the address."

"I...are you sure?"

"Yeah. We need the privacy. And I want to be alone with you. Sending a text. See you in a minute."

The line went dead. A few seconds later, my phone buzzed with his address.

I plugged it into my GPS and pulled out of the garage.

Chapter Eleven

HARPER

The door swung open, revealing Cole in jeans and a t-shirt, the light from the house spilling out around him in the doorway. Whatever he read in my expression made his shoulders tense slightly—the subtle reaction of a man who recognized trouble when it arrived on his doorstep.

"Come on in," he said, stepping aside.

The inside of his house was clean and functional, but also warm and lived-in. Hardwood floors stretched through the space. A comfortable-looking couch faced a flat screen TV. A coffee table held a few medical journals stacked neatly. Bookcases lined one wall, filled with textbooks and what looked like fiction mixed in. Colorful abstract art hung on the walls alongside a few framed family photos. The space felt like him—simple but welcoming, minimal without being sterile, comfortable without being cluttered.

"You need something to drink?" Cole asked, leading me toward the kitchen. "Water? Beer? I might have a bottle of wine, but I'm partial to brown liquor. I'm not much of a drinker at home, so the options are limited."

"Water's fine," I said, following him into the kitchen. "For now."

He filled a glass from the filtered dispenser in the refrigerator door. The kitchen was spotless, all white counters and stainless steel appliances. A dish towel was folded over the handle of the oven. Either Cole had a hell of a housekeeper or he was compulsively neat.

"So," he said, handing me the glass. His eyes tracked over my face again, more careful this time. "I know what happened at the meeting but tell me about the meeting."

I took a long sip of ice-cold water, then set the glass down on the counter.

"The meeting was shit," I said. "It didn't start off shit, but I did my presentation, shared every detail, all of your notes. And then..."

I shook my head.

"Ambush."

"Exactly. They were just nitpicking about how many times we tried to call next of kin. It just...that man was dying. He was dying no matter what. She was three fucking hours away and she didn't check her voicemail? She couldn't send someone local to be with him? Just..."

I heaved a sigh. Cole gestured toward the water glass. I sucked down another swallow.

"Then out of left field, they started asking who made the decision to operate and did you consult anyone and couldn't you have waited and suddenly, they want to talk to the surgeon. Like that's ever a reasonable request."

"Oh, that's the whole reason for the meeting," said Cole. "It was always going to end up that way."

"Yeah, well. Instead of anyone but me taking up for you, admin and Legal agreed that you should be at the next meeting."

Cole nodded slowly. His expression didn't change, didn't register surprise or anger or anything I expected. "Yeah, Dr. Webb told me."

I stared at him, searching for some crack in that calm exterior. "And?"

"And what?"

"And I want you to be pissed like I am!" My voice shot up, higher and louder than I'd intended. I had made a promise to myself to stay calm, to keep my cool, to just say things like a normal person.

That promise lasted about two seconds.

"I want you to tell me you're not going to let them do this to you. I want you to—"

My words cut off, snagged in my throat. My head was pounding, the bun I'd twisted up this morning now pulling at my scalp, making everything worse.

My fingers clawed at my hair, finding one bobby pin, then another. Cole stepped in and caught my hand. "Hold on."

He moved in close behind me, taking over, sliding the pins free one by one. Then he tugged the elastic band around the bun loose and pulled it free, his fingers working through the tight coil at the back of my head until the tension gave way and my hair fell loose around my shoulders.

I sighed in instant relief. "Go on," said Cole.

"Rachel Gaines found a gap in the timeline," I continued. "I mean, not a real gap, just something she could twist into looking like negligence. She made it sound like we didn't try hard enough to reach the family."

I started pacing his kitchen, unable to stand still. The nervous energy had to go somewhere.

"And now she wants Diane Hart to paint you as reckless, as someone who prioritized a procedure over humanity."

Cole leaned against the counter, arms folded tight across his chest, watching me pace as if everything he'd built wasn't about to get dragged out into the open and torn apart by strangers' hands. He took it the way someone might absorb news of a change in weather: mild interest, no panic, no sign of the storm I knew was coming.

"What did you say to that?" he asked.

"Of course I told them no."

I stopped pacing and turned to face him. Cole pushed off the counter and closed the distance, his hands settling on my shoulders. His thumbs pressed in just enough to ease the tension still sitting there.

I exhaled, some of the edge bleeding off. For a second, I let myself lean into him, my forehead brushing his chest before I straightened again.

"I told Rachel, I told Adrienne, I told Gerald, Dr. Webb, Dr. Rice. I said putting you in a room with the family was setting you up to fail and it sounded like they were building a case for malpractice."

"And?"

"And it was like I wasn't talking. Liz said you could appear at the next meeting and Webb agreed with her, and Legal was just like, 'that seems like a reasonable request.' Complete bullshit."

Cole's lips twitched, but he didn't smile. "All that matters is what they can spin. You know that."

"Yeah, I know that. But also fuck that." I slammed my palm on the counter, hard enough to rattle the glass. "And how are you so damn calm? Am I...am I wrong here?"

"No," Cole said. "You're not wrong at all. You're upset at my lack of emotion like I haven't been anticipating this since Dr. Webb called me to tell me Risk was bringing this back up."

"Yes!" The word burst out of me, loud in the quiet kitchen. "You are severely under-reacting to the fact that they're going to crucify you. Dr. Rice told me to my face that if this goes bad, you're on your own. They'll cut you loose and let you take the blame. And Diane Hart..."

I shook my head. "She *acts* guilty. Not just sad, but *guilty*. She does a good job of letting her lawyer be the pit bull, but she was out of town when her grandfather died. And not just out of town but not reachable for hours. And now she needs someone to blame because she can't live with the fact that she wasn't there when it happened. Rachel Gaines is smart enough to use that guilt, to channel it into anger. She'll make you the villain in this story and there won't be anything I can do to stop it."

"Yep," Cole said, so matter-of-fact it made me want to scream. "I figured this is how it would end up."

"You figured," I repeated, my voice flat. "You figured this is how it would go, so you're just...what? Accepting it? Giving up?"

"Harper."

Cole's tone was even, steady, but his eyes darkened the way a room dims when a cloud passes overhead. "I've been a Black surgeon for twenty years. This isn't my first questionable death. I knew that was part of the deal when I accepted the job at RMC. I'd make that call again. Every time."

"Knowing it's going to happen doesn't make it right."

"No," he agreed. "It doesn't. But it's reality. And getting angry about reality doesn't change the game. It makes you play worse."

I opened my mouth to argue, then closed it again. My hands were shaking. I pressed them flat against the cool granite countertop. "Dr. Rice threatened my job," I said quietly.

For the first time since I'd walked in, Cole's composure slipped. His brows knit together. "What?"

"After the meeting today. She told me that if I don't fall in line, I'm not a fit for this role." I laughed, but there was no humor in it. The sound came out bitter and harsh. "She said I'm not thinking strategically. That my job is to protect the hospital, not you. That I'm letting my personal feelings cloud my professional judgment."

"She's not wrong," Cole said, with a tilt to his head.

"Cole—"

"Where is the lie?" he insisted, cutting me off. "You can't put your career on the line for me. I won't let you do that."

"You won't let me?" I moved away from him, anger flaring in my chest. "You don't get to decide that for me."

"What do you want me to say, Harper?" Cole's voice rose for the first time. "It's okay if you lose everything you've worked for because RMC administration is playing politics with my career? We don't have to go down together. I don't want that. I won't accept that."

"So, what am I supposed to do? Watch them tear you apart?"

"If that's what it takes to keep your job—"

"Cole, that's bullshit."

"That's reality."

There was that word again. Reality. I realized I was beginning to hate it.

Cole stepped close again, enough that I could feel his body heat, sense his heartbeat. It was soothing, in a way. His tone dropped lower, softer.

"I appreciate that you're concerned. I love that you want to fight for me. But I've been handling situations like this my entire career. You don't need to sacrifice yourself to save me."

"What if I want to?"

His hand slid up my side, across my shoulder, up my neck until he cupped my cheek in his palm. "Don't want to. I'm not worth losing everything for."

"If this were anyone else, I'd still want to do what's right. But it's you—a skilled, talented Black surgeon. And that makes it different, and you know why. I don't have the luxury of pretending it doesn't."

"I know, baby. I know."

He stepped even closer, backing me against the island until I was pinned between the counter and his body. Then he dipped his head and dropped his lips to mine. The relief I felt at being near him, touching him, kissing him, was overwhelming. My whole body exhaled tension I hadn't realized I was carrying.

Let me find out all I needed was a man to kiss me and suddenly the world made sense again.

Within seconds, the kiss was a deep, groaning frenzy, his hands in my hair, fingers tangling in the curls I'd just freed. I grabbed fistfuls of his t-shirt and pulled it up, needing to feel him under my palms. I found warm, smooth skin and the rapid thump of his heartbeat.

Cole's hands moved to my blouse, working the buttons open. He pushed the fabric off my shoulders and let it flutter to the floor. Then his mouth was on my neck, my collarbone, trailing heat everywhere he touched.

"Cole, we haven't—"

"I know." He was already reaching for the zipper to my skirt. "This is not what you came over here for. If you want me to stop, I will. But if you don't want me to stop, then let me take some stress off your shoulders. Then we can talk about what we do next."

I was a sucker if I ever saw one, but I didn't care.

We shed clothes fast—my skirt hitting the floor, his jeans following, items discarded in a trail from the kitchen to the living room and eventually the large, plush couch.

This wasn't like the desperate fuck in the supply closet at the hospital. This was need and release and two people trying to forget the outside world for just a little while.

His hand slid down my body, fingers hooking into the waistband of my panties. He paused, looking up at me with a wicked grin. "If I have to take these off, I'm adding them to my collection."

"Oh, hell no," I managed to say, though I was rapidly losing the ability to form coherent thought. "You cannot keep all of my expensive unmentionables, Cole."

I lifted my hips and pulled them off before he could confiscate them. His hands trailed over my thighs as the fabric slid down my legs. Then he was kissing lower—my ribs, my stomach, my inner thighs.

When his tongue ghosted my clit, I couldn't hold back the guttural moan that tore from my throat. His hands gripped my thighs firmly, holding me open and exposed to him.

Every time I got close to the edge, close enough that I could feel my orgasm building like a wave about to crest, he'd slow down or change rhythm. He kept me hovering on that knife's edge between pleasure and release for so long I wanted to cry.

"Cole, please!" I begged, my fingers gripping his skin.

"Mmmhmmm," he hummed, and I felt the vibration all the way up to my core.

Finally, mercifully, his mouth sealed over my clit, sucking with steady pressure while his fingers pushed inside me. They curled to hit that spot deep inside that made me see stars and practically levitate.

I came so hard my vision blurred, my body shuddering in his grasp. I heard myself crying out, his name tangled up with a string of words that barely sounded like English. Cole held me through the aftershocks, his mouth gentling, then kissing light as rain along my trembling thighs.

Only when my breathing slowed did he move up to lie beside me, cradling my head against his chest. His heart was hammering as loud as mine. I realized, a little dazedly, that he hadn't even taken himself out of his boxers. I dove for him and, before he could stop me, pulled him free, wrapping my hand around his thick length, marveling at the flush of it, the velvet heat, the way he shuddered when I stroked him.

He let out a ragged groan as I took him. I craved that sound, the tremor that ran through him, the way his whole body tensed, as if he was fighting to keep himself from losing control.

I loved being in this position, asserting this much power over his body and this moment.

His hands fisted in the couch cushions, his jaw locked against whatever sounds wanted to escape, and when I ran my tongue along the underside of his dick, he exhaled a shaky groan that felt like a little victory.

He tried to gently guide my rhythm, one hand on the

back of my head, but I ignored it, taking him deeper, working him with my mouth and hands until he bucked, beginning a slow, rhythmic roll.

I wanted to taste his surrender, wanted to make him come. Hard.

"Hey," he whispered, pulling me from him. I thought I'd done something wrong until I saw the hunger in his eyes. "Not that this isn't mind-blowing, but I want to be inside you when I come. You ready for me?"

I was ready for him in ways I didn't even have words for. My body was still pulsing from the aftershocks of the orgasm, nerves alive and skin hypersensitive to every point of contact between us. "Yeah," I whispered, lying back, fingers clutching at him to come near me, needing the feel of him, the weight and heat and everything.

He grinned, then stripped off his boxer briefs and sank between my thighs. The solid weight of him pressing me into the couch was so intense I thought I might shatter. His hands gripped my hips, anchoring us.

"Look at me," he said, his voice pitched low, rough.

I opened my eyes and met his gaze. The intensity there stole what little breath I'd managed to recover.

"I've got you," he said. And then his hips rolled forward in a slow, deliberate thrust, followed by long, deep strokes that hit every nerve ending like he'd studied a map of my body.

I clawed at him, my nails digging into his skin hard enough to leave marks. He groaned at the sensation, his movements quickening, deepening, driving into me with an intensity that tore his name from my throat with each breath.

"Don't...stop..." I chanted, my voice breaking into a staccato rhythm. I could feel myself climbing toward another peak and I needed more. Every muscle, every cell was electrified, driven by a single animalistic need.

Cole curled his hand behind my knee and lifted my leg, bracing my calf over his shoulder. The motion was a counterpoint to the wild, relentless force of his hips, but when the new angle let him sink even deeper, I let out a sound that would have scared me if I didn't realize it came from my body.

"It's good, huh? You like that? You like how I fuck this pussy, Harper?"

It was all I could do to nod, my mouth falling open as Cole's teeth grazed my collarbone, and then he was kissing me, open-mouthed and wild while he drove into me with a punishing rhythm. I felt myself unravel, the wave rising again, higher and higher. I was close, so close, and he could tell.

He slowed, then snapped his hips in a hard thrust that made my whole body convulse. "I need to feel you come."

"You already know me well enough to know what I need," I shot back.

He grinned, clearly enjoying my sass, and slipped a hand between our bodies. His thumb found my clit and the added stimulation was too much. My eyes locked on his face, watching every shadow that crossed his features.

"Cole! Oh my God! Oh, fuck, I'm gonna—"

"Yeah. Me too, gorgeous. Come on, girl. We'll go together."

With a guttural cry, every muscle in my body went rigid, fire streaking through me as I pulsed around him. I couldn't speak, only gasp his name over and over, barely enunciating the syllables.

Cole shuddered, a long, drawn out, "Yessss..." spilling from his clenched teeth. His thrusts turned into hard, quick bursts like he was chasing a high. I forced breath into my lungs, still trembling, the aftershocks still making me shiver.

He buried himself deep and released with a groan that was all surrender. He chanted my name against my neck, the tension arcing through his body until he was spent.

Cole grew limp and collapsed, his body a large, hot, heavy blanket I never wanted to kick off. He immediately pulled me against him so that I was draped across his chest.

I giggled, the sound bubbling up from somewhere deep in my chest. I looked up at him, propping my chin on his sternum.

"When are we projected to make it to a bed?"

* * *

"I heard you earlier," I said quietly.

After we actually made it to his bed and enjoyed each other again, we rested in a tangled and sweaty heap. I lay across his body, head on his chest.

"When?" Cole mumbled.

"You know, before you grounded me with a good fucking."

He snorted. "Had to calm them histrionics, girl. Get your head on straight."

"Yeah, whatever," I said, landing a light slap to his skin. "I'm serious. I want to protect you—I need to protect you. I don't know how."

Cole's hand stroked slow paths up and down my back. "You don't have to protect me. You need to protect yourself."

"It's not fair to you to focus on myself."

"Life's not fair, Harper. You know that better than most people."

I did know that. But I didn't have to like it. And I didn't ever think I could live by it.

This put Cole and me at the softest, most gentle of impasses.

Finally I sat up, kicking the sheets off my legs. "I need to go."

"Harper." Cole sat up too, reaching for me. "Are you mad at me? Because I don't want you to risk your job for me?"

"No, I'm not mad." I looked at him, really looked at him in the dim light filtering through his bedroom window. "I'm not mad at you, anyway. I need some time to think about how I can do my job without sacrificing you in the process. I can't do that. I won't do that."

Cole watched me for another moment, then nodded and got up. He pulled on a pair of cotton lounge pants and walked with me back to the kitchen, where he picked up my scattered clothing, item by item, and I pulled each piece back on. My blouse. My skirt. My bra.

Everything except my panties, which Cole had managed to confiscate.

"I reiterate that you don't have to go," he said, leaning against the door frame, arms crossed over his bare chest. "I can make you a hell of a protein shake. I got some chicken in the fridge. I could throw together some pasta."

I chuckled, buttoning the last button on my blouse. "I thank you for the hospitality. And by hospitality, I mean that vibranium dick. I don't know where you've been hiding that particular asset, but I'm about to take out an insurance policy on it."

"You're silly." He pushed off the door frame and pulled me into his arms. "Come back when you can stay longer."

"Don't play with me, Cole."

He kissed me then, slow and sweet, in a way that said he really didn't want me to leave. His hands cupped my ass, pulling me close enough to feel him hardening again.

"Wait until you find out I'm really not playing with you, Harper," he said against my lips. "Text me when you get home."

I drove home through streets as empty as my thoughts were crowded, possibilities and strategies stacking up in my head. By the time I swung into my parking spot, I realized what I'd decided already, somewhere between Cole's place and mine.

Ridgeway Medical Center was going to set Cole up as the fall guy. That was beyond my control. So was whatever Rice, Webb, or Legal decided to do with him.

But I could make sure Cole was ready for that meeting. And not just ready—incredibly, painfully over-prepared.

I headed inside, dropped my bag by the door, and went straight for my laptop, setting it on the kitchen counter. I made a pot of coffee, changed into a pair of sweats, then perched at the counter and opened a blank document. My fingers hovered over the keys for a second, then I started typing.

There was something I could do.

Chapter Twelve

C OLE

An email from Dr. Webb hit my inbox at 05:08.

MARCUS WEBB:

IMPORTANT: Please come by my office this afternoon, re: the upcoming Hart meeting.

I stared at the timestamp, picturing him hunched over his keyboard at too damn early in the morning, either buried in administrative work or wrestling with insomnia. Neither scenario suggested good news awaited me.

Harper had left my place a few hours before that, her taillights disappearing down my street while I stood in the doorway watching. I'd spent the rest of the night replaying every moment with her instead of sleeping, wondering if I'd read too much into her lingering kiss goodnight or the way she'd hesitated before leaving.

I knocked on Dr. Webb's door after I'd finished my day. His gruff, "Come in," sounded even more weathered than usual. He looked up when I settled into the chair across from his desk.

"Cole. Thanks for coming in."

"You said it was important," I replied, implying that I didn't really have a choice.

"Indeed, it is." He set the tablet down, folded his hands on top of it, the way people do when they're about to say something you're not going to like. "I wanted to touch base about Tuesday's meeting. Make sure you're ready."

I shrugged, like there was nothing to it. "What's to be ready for?"

"This meeting is critical. The Hart family has considerable influence with the Board, and we need to handle this delicately."

I caught the word *delicately*. Honestly, all I saw was the same old boardroom politics, just with fancier names and a little more glass in the conference room. Webb wanted us walking on eggshells; I wasn't sure why we couldn't just walk in, confident that we were in the right.

Still, I got it. The Hart family had pull, and if we blew it, we'd feel it.

"Just remember, Dr. Vaughn. At this point, this isn't about being right. It's about being diplomatic."

"I was right, though. The decision to operate was correct given the clinical presentation."

"I know that. You know that." Webb spread his hands in a gesture that was supposed to look reassuring but came off as placating. "But Mrs. Hart doesn't know that. She's grieving. She's angry. She needs someone to help her make sense of what happened. Help her understand that Mr. Greene's death wasn't due to negligence or poor judgment."

Webb's voice took on an edge. "That's all anyone is asking, Cole."

"Is it, though?" I leaned in, resting my elbows on my knees. "Because it sounds like you're asking me to fall on my sword. Apologize for not doing something I wouldn't normally do."

"No one is asking you to apologize, Cole."

"Let's get clear, then. What are you asking?"

Webb was quiet for a moment. When he spoke again, his voice had shifted into what I recognized as the tone he used when someone was being difficult. "I'm asking you to be mindful of how you present yourself. The family's attorney is going to try to provoke you. She's going to ask pointed questions designed to make you defensive or appear arrogant. I'm asking you to remain calm and professional and not give her ammunition."

"I can do that."

"Can you?" Webb's eyebrows rose. "Because I've seen you in meetings that don't turn out friendly. You don't suffer fools. You don't hide your opinions. And right now, we need you to think carefully about how you come across."

"So, don't be the big, scary Black man in the room?"

"Believe it or not, I'm on your side."

"It doesn't feel like it, Dr. Webb. This lawyer is going to twist my words until I sound like the villain. And I'm supposed to just take it."

Webb's jaw flexed. I watched him recalibrate, searching for the right response.

"Look," he finally said, leaning back in his chair. "I'm not asking you to grovel or admit fault where none exists. What I'm asking is that you remember that perception matters as much as reality in situations like this. Mrs. Hart lost her grandfather. She's looking for answers. If we can't provide them in a way that feels compassionate, she's going to assume we're hiding something."

Webb's voice dropped lower, taking on the tone of someone sharing hard wisdom. "Cole, you're a talented surgeon. You have a bright future. Don't throw it away by being stubborn in one meeting."

I stood. "If defending sound medical judgment makes me stubborn, then I guess that's what I am."

"Cole—"

"I wasn't wrong. And I'm not going to pretend I was to make the Hart family feel better or to keep the Board happy or to protect the hospital's donor relationships." I moved to the door. "If that's what you need from me, Dr. Webb, then we have a problem."

"Sit down, son."

I stopped, hand on the doorknob. "I'm not your son, Dr. Webb. And you might be the department head, but watch how you speak to me."

Webb's face went through several expressions—surprise, then something that might have been hurt, before settling into the careful neutrality he wore during difficult surgeries. We stood facing each other across his desk.

"Alright, listen," he said. "I understand you're frustrated. I understand this feels unfair. But you need to understand something too—this isn't about you. It's about the entire department. If the Hart family decides to make an issue of this, it doesn't just affect you. It affects our funding, our reputation, our ability to recruit top talent."

"So I should take one for the team."

"We all have to be team players sometimes." His hands pressed flat against the desk. "Do I think it's fair that you're being put in this position? No. Do I think the hospital should be backing you more forcefully? Yes. But that's not the reality we're dealing with."

"What did they offer you?" I asked quietly.

Webb's brown eyes blinked rapidly. "What?"

"To make sure I stay in line. What did they offer you? A bonus? A raise? More vacation? Or what did they threaten you with?"

"Cole, that's out of line—"

"I know how this works. Administration never leaves anything to chance. They would have approached you, made sure you understood what's at stake. Made sure you understood that your job is to manage me."

Webb's face went carefully blank. "No one offered me anything."

"But they talked to you."

The silence stretched long enough to be an answer.

"Legal?" I suggested. "Dr. Rice? Higher? Chairman, maybe?"

"There was a conversation about how to support you through this situation."

"Right. Support me by making sure I don't rock the boat, say all the right things, bend over for the rich folk so they'll keep giving us money."

Webb's jaw worked. "Cole, you're making this more complicated than it needs to be."

"No, you're making it simple when it shouldn't be." I pulled the door open. "Thanks for the prep session, Dr. Webb."

"Dr. Vaughn—"

I walked out before he could finish.

The hallway was empty, just carpeted floors and closed doors with nameplates announcing the occupants' names and titles. I took the stairs down instead of the elevator, needing the physical movement to burn off the anger building in my chest.

My office was nothing like Webb's—no mahogany desk, no leather chairs, no view. Just a functional space with a computer, a filing cabinet, and a secondhand bookshelf I'd picked up from a resident who was moving across the country. But it was mine, and more importantly, it was private.

I closed the door, dropped into my desk chair, pulled up my VIP contact list and scrolled to a number. The call connected on the third ring.

"Cole! Caught me between meetings! Everything alright?"

My stepfather, Walter Ellis, had a voice that immediately eased some of the tension in my shoulders, even over the phone line. The Ellis Clinic specialized in executive health services and taught him how to navigate the intersection of medicine and money better than anyone I knew.

"Hey, Dad. You got a minute?"

"Always. What's going on?"

I leaned back in my chair, staring at the ceiling tiles. "I need some advice. Might lean toward the legal area, actually."

There was a pause. "Legal? Son...what's happening?"

I gave him the abbreviated version of the story, starting with Earl Greene in the ER and ending with the upcoming meeting. Dad listened without interrupting, letting me get it all out before weighing in.

"And Dr. Webb's direction is to capitulate?"

"Pretty much. Play nice, don't make waves, help the grieving family understand that nobody did anything wrong —but if we did do something wrong, it wasn't the hospital's fault."

"Which means they're positioning you as expendable."

"That's my understanding."

Dad was quiet for a long moment. I could picture him in his office, leaning back in an expensive leather desk chair, fingers steepled while he processed what I'd told him. "Have they told you that you need legal representation?"

"No. But Harp—someone suggested I shouldn't answer questions without a representative present."

"Someone..." Dad echoed, and there was an edge now, a flick of curiosity. "Does this someone work for the hospital?"

"Yes. The case came up through Risk Management."

He didn't say anything right away. I could feel him on the other end, the gears in his mind turning. "So someone from Risk Management is advising you? A Black surgeon in the middle of an investigation that involves donors?"

"...yeah."

"Son."

I tried to sidestep it. "Dad, I don't—"

"Is she a Black woman?"

I paused. No point in pretending, no point in dressing it up as anything but what it was. Harper Sutton was gorgeous, brilliant, sharp as a scalpel—and yes, a Black woman. I was losing my head over her, fast.

"Yeah."

A deep bellow of laughter sounded over the line. "Now it makes sense. Risk Management doesn't stick their neck out for anybody, much less for one of us. She sounds special."

"She is."

"Mmhmm. We'll definitely come back to that," he said, and I could practically see the smile on his face through the phone. "But yes, you need an attorney. Not because you did anything wrong but because despite that, the hospital seems poised to place the blame on your shoulders, which opens you up to liability issues down the line. You want someone who can make sure you don't inadvertently say something that could be used against you later."

"That's what I figured."

"Let me call Vincent Cross," he suggested. "He's a malpractice defense attorney out of Atlanta, but he takes cases nationally. He handled a situation for a colleague of mine a few years back. Brilliant strategist, doesn't back down from hospitals or their legal teams."

"Sounds good. I'd appreciate an introduction."

"Of course. Now listen, Cole." He paused. "I know this is hard. I know it feels like everything you've worked for is being used against you. But you made the right call. Don't let them railroad you into doubting that."

I choked up at that. "That's the thing—the doublespeak I'm dealing with. Like Dr. Webb agrees I did the right thing, that they have no issues with the decisions I made, but also at the first mention of trouble, I'm the problem and they need me to admit that."

"Webb is covering his ass. That's what department chairs do when they've been at it too long—they forget what it's like to actually practice medicine, to only have a few seconds to make a decision. They get comfortable in their corner offices and forget that real doctors are down in the trenches making life-and-death decisions every day."

"Yeah. Exactly."

"Cole, are you listening to me? Ears open?"

"Wide open. I'm listening."

"Good. Because I need you to hear this—you did nothing wrong. You made a judgment call; that patient's family wasn't there and you couldn't wait. Any reasonable surgeon would have made the same call."

"I know."

"Then act like you know it. When you walk into that meeting Tuesday, you walk in with your head up. You answer their questions professionally and honestly. You don't apologize for saving lives, and you don't let them twist your decisions into something they weren't."

I closed my eyes, letting his words settle. "Thanks, Dad."

"Now." He paused and I felt my eyes beginning to roll. "Tell me about this Black woman in Risk Management."

I couldn't help my smile, knowing full well it was translating to my voice. "Her name is Harper."

"Harper," Dad repeated, as if he was rolling a rare coin between his fingers. "That's a good, strong name. And this Harper is going out on a limb for you?"

"She's trying to. It's...You know what it's like when most of the staff doesn't look like you. We connected on that level pretty early and she warned me that this was a track the hospital might take."

"Mmmmh," he hummed, appearing to contemplate my words. "Are you personally involved?"

"Officially, absolutely not. The most professional of relationships."

"And unofficially?"

I didn't know what to say. Harper and I weren't dating, but we'd been out together and spent time together and had definitely crossed a few lines that we shouldn't have crossed. But I also didn't regret crossing them.

"It's complicated," I finally said.

"I bet it is. Hospital politics always are, especially when you mix in personal feelings."

"I ain't said nothin' about—"

"Son, I've been married to your mother long enough to

know. It's in your voice." He paused. "You need to be careful. If this goes sideways, she could get caught up."

"I know. That's what I'm worried about."

"Then make sure you both come out of this intact. I'll have Vincent reach out to you. Prepare for that meeting. And make sure Harper keeps her head up high too. Call me after the meeting Tuesday. I want to hear how it goes. Oh, and son?"

"Yeah, Dad?"

"The next family FaceTime session, make sure Harper is around. I'd like to lay my eyes on her. Your mother would sure love to meet the woman who may have tamed her youngest boy."

I laughed despite everything. "We're not—it's not like that."

"Yet," Dad said. "Keep me in the loop. On everything."

"I will, Dad."

I hung up and sat there for a moment, phone still in my hand. Dad had spent years as a physician, many of those at a major teaching hospital. He'd navigated the same politics, the same bureaucracy, the same careful dance between doing your job and keeping administration happy. If he said I needed an attorney, I needed an attorney.

And if he thought Harper was worth meeting, then what was happening between us was more than just complicated.

My phone buzzed with a text before I could think too hard about that.

BANKS:

Hey Vaughn. We missed you last night. Plastics beat our asses. Where'd you get off to?

I stared at the message for a moment, debating how to respond.

ME:

Had something come up.

BANKS:

Mmhmm. You playing tonight? We need to reclaim our crown.

ME:

It's Wednesday, Banks.

BANKS:

I know what the hell day it is, man. We play when we play. You in or out?

I needed to burn off the tension from this morning. I needed to stop replaying Webb's words in my head.

ME:

Gimme thirty minutes.

I changed quickly, trading my button-down and slacks for shorts and a t-shirt that had seen better days. The fabric was worn soft from too many washes, the hospital logo on the front faded to almost nothing.

The gym was more crowded than I expected for a Wednesday evening. Both courts were in use—cardio had claimed one end for a pick-up game of their own, and trauma had the other. I spotted Banks immediately, already warming up with Dr. Kim and a few others I recognized from Tuesday nights.

Banks was five foot nine, built like an athlete, with deep brown skin and a fade that was always crisp. She spent her high school and college years playing competitive sports, from lacrosse to basketball to soccer. Her hands were quick, her court sense was excellent, and she talked more shit during a game than anyone I'd ever met.

"Vaughn!" Kim called when he saw me. "You lost? This isn't Tuesday."

"I know what day it is."

"Mans missed a day, so I made him come down tonight," Banks said, jogging over with a grin splitting her face. She dribbled the ball between her legs, showing off. "We got our asses handed to us by plastics. *Plastics*, Cole. Do you know how embarrassing that is?"

"Sounds like a you problem."

"Sounds like a *we* problem since you weren't there to carry us." She tossed me the ball. "So where were you? And don't say work because I checked the board."

I caught the ball, took a shot from the three-point line. It rimmed out. "Had something to take care of."

"Something." Banks retrieved the ball, passed it back to me. "Or someone?"

"Banks—"

"Because word around the hospital is you've been spending a lot of time on the ICU floor lately. And the ICU floor just happens to be where a certain director of Risk Management does a lot of her work." Her eyebrows hiked curiously. "Funny coincidence, that."

"You're reading into things."

"Am I?" Banks moved closer, lowering her voice. "Because I saw you and Harper Sutton in the hallway last week. The way you two were looking at each other was not professional, Vaughn."

I took another shot. This one went in. "We have a professional relationship."

"Mmhmm. *Professional*." Banks laughed. "You don't

look at anybody at work the way you were looking at her. And she was definitely looking back."

"Even if that were true—shit's complicated."

"Yeah, it is. She works for the hospital. You're in the middle of the Greene investigation. That's like, maximum complicated." Banks dribbled past me, sank an easy layup. "But that's not what I'm asking about. I'm asking if you're finally letting yourself have something good."

"What's that supposed to mean?"

"It means you've been married to this place since I met you. Early mornings, late nights, weekends in the OR. No hobbies except basketball once a week. No relationships. No life outside these walls."

She grabbed the ball, held it against her hip. "Harper Sutton is smart, super fine, and from what I've seen, she's got backbone. You should be so lucky to get some of her time. Don't sabotage it because you're scared."

"I am not scared."

"Then what are you?"

I didn't have a good answer for that. Banks waited, watching me with those eyes that missed nothing.

"The Greene case is going to get worse before it gets better," I said finally. "If Harper and I—if there's something there, it puts her in a difficult position."

"So you're trying to protect her."

"By not dragging her down with me if this goes sideways."

Banks shook her head. "Man, that's some tragic hero bullshit. She knows what she's doing."

"This is different. The Hart family has serious pull with the Board. If they decide to make an example of me, anyone close to me becomes collateral damage."

"And you think Harper doesn't know that?" Banks

stepped closer. "Cole, listen. If she's looking out for you, it's because she chose to. She has a reason to. Don't insult her by assuming she can't handle her business."

"I'm not—"

"You *are.* You're doing that thing where you decide what's best for everyone else without asking them. It's annoying when you do it with residents, and it's gotta be annoying when you do it with women you're sleeping with."

"I never said I was—"

"Boy, you ain't have to." Banks grinned. "Your energy screams that y'all been fucking. Don't even try to tell me you just be having some good conversations. Good conversations, my ass."

I opened my mouth to argue, then closed it. There was no point. Banks had already figured it out.

"So...what?" I asked. "What do I say now?"

"Say you're going to stop trying to be a martyr and let someone be on your team. Say you're going to fight for yourself and for whatever's happening between you and Harper, instead of sacrificing yourself because you think that's noble."

"I'm not sacrificing myself. I'm fighting. I just don't want her caught up in whatever's going to happen to me."

Kim and a few others had drifted to the far end of the court, giving us space. I nodded downcourt and gave them two fingers, meaning give us a couple of minutes.

"Look, I like her, okay?" I said finally. "More than I expected to. More than I should, given the circumstances."

Banks's grin softened into something more genuine. "Good. You deserve some happiness in your life."

"But if this goes badly—"

"Then you deal with it together. That's how relationships

work, Cole. You don't get to decide unilaterally that you're going to take all the damage so she doesn't have to. That's not protecting her. That's just you being a control freak."

I couldn't help but laugh. "Tell me how you really feel."

"I'm always gon' be real." Banks punched my shoulder. "Harper's grown. Real grown. Let her make her own choices. If one of those choices is *you*, don't fuck it up."

I sucked my teeth. "So much easier said than done."

"Everything worth having is. Ask me how I know." Banks winked, then tossed me the ball. "Now can we please work off the humiliation of losing to plastics?"

I smirked. "Y'all lost to sorry ass plastics and now it's my problem?"

"Yes. Now we beat them so badly they never want to play us again."

We played three games. Trauma won two out of three, with me scoring the winning basket in the final game. By the time we were done, everyone was heaving hard breaths and dripping sweat.

"That's more like it," Banks said, high-fiving Kim. "Trauma's back on top."

I showered in the locker room and changed back into my street clothes. The parking garage was mostly empty, just a few cars scattered across the levels. I was halfway to my car when I saw her.

Bag slung over her shoulder, phone pressed to her ear, she looked exhausted—shoulders tight, face drawn. She was nodding at whatever the person on the other end was saying, her free hand rubbing her temple like she was fighting off a headache.

She hadn't seen me yet. I could get in my car, drive away, give her space.

But watching her walk alone through the garage, looking like the weight of the world was pressing down on her shoulders... I couldn't just leave.

I changed direction, heading toward her car instead of mine. She looked up as I got close, her eyes widening slightly. She said something into the phone—an excuse to get off—then lowered it.

"Cole...uhm, hi."

"Hey. You alright?" I asked. "You look..."

"Like it was a long day?" She slipped her phone into her bag. "Yeah. You?"

"Had a fun conversation with Webb this afternoon."

"Shit." Harper glanced around the garage, checking for cameras, for people, for witnesses. Finding none, she moved closer. "How bad was it?"

"Bad enough. He made it clear the hospital expects me to play nice on Tuesday."

"Did he at least pretend to have your back?"

"For a minute. Then it became clear he's more worried about keeping his corner office than supporting his surgeons."

Harper's expression darkened. "I'm sorry. You deserve better than that."

"It is what it is." I shifted my weight, suddenly aware of how close we were standing. How alone we were. How much I wanted to close the remaining distance between us. "I talked to my dad afterward. He's connecting me with an attorney."

"Good." Her expression brightened. "I...I think that's a good move. You shouldn't alert anyone ahead of time that you've retained counsel. I've been working on prep materials for you—questions they're likely to ask, how to frame your answers, what landmines to avoid. It would be a good thing to go over with your attorney."

"You didn't have to do that."

"Yes, I did." Her voice dropped lower. "I meant what I said. I'm not letting them sacrifice you."

"Harper—"

She cut me off, stepping closer still. "And I know what Dr. Rice said to me, what the stakes are for both of us. But I'm not backing down on this."

"Harper, I gotta tell you something."

"Sure."

"It's killing me that I'm standing here in this parking lot at work when I want you in my arms. When I want to kiss the shit out of those lips, cameras be damned. When I just want to hold you and tell you that you're the first person in a long time to make me feel like I'm not fighting alone. I'm just so tired of feeling like I'm alone, and I really appreciate you being an absolute dog with a fucking bone about this right now."

"I, uhm. You...shit." She stuttered, then laughed, stomping a cute little booted foot. "The fuck am I supposed to say to that, Cole?"

"You're supposed to tell me you have time for me tonight."

She looked at me for a long moment, her teeth worrying her bottom lip. I could see her thinking, weighing options, calculating risks.

"It just so happens," she finally said, "that I have about two tons of food that my mother sent me home with. Beef roast, mac and cheese, greens, cornbread. More than I can eat by myself."

My brows rose a little higher at every new mention of food. "Sounds incredible."

"It is. The problem is she can only cook for thirty people." She pulled her keys from her bag. "I'll text you my address. We can go through the prep materials while we eat."

"*Just* go over prep materials?"

"Well..." Her smile turned into something warmer, more intimate. "We could pick up where we left off. If you're interested."

"I'm interested. What can I bring?"

She closed the space between us, then stood on her tiptoes to whisper in my ear.

"My *goddamn* panties."

Chapter Thirteen

COLE

I awoke to the warmth of a palm around me, sliding up and down in slow, measured passes.

The pressure was perfect—a little tighter mid-stroke, then easing off near the tip, her thumb circling there before she started over again. Sometimes she'd let go completely, fingers wandering up over my stomach, tracing lines across my chest, leaving a lingering heat in their wake before returning to wrap around me once more.

I blinked my eyes open, disoriented for the briefest of moments. The softness of Harper's body pressed into mine answered the question before I could ask myself where I was. She was curled in beside me, her breasts smashed against my chest, one of her thighs tossed across mine, her mound plastered against my hip and, ever so slowly, rocking against the bone.

The sheets had wriggled their way down in the night, so we were naked, sprawled out together. Her legs were bare, smooth as silk, every little move she made sparking a fresh wave of arousal, edging me closer to being fully awake.

The room was still dark, the faintest hint of gray light coming through the curtains, so it was early. Too early for her neighbors to appreciate the kind of noise I wanted to make.

"Morning," she whispered against my neck, her breath tickling my skin. I bit back a groan as her hand continued its slow torture.

"Well, good morning. What time is it?"

"Five thirty. I wasn't sure what time you get up for work." She kissed my jaw, my throat, working her way down. "But I didn't figure you'd be mad if I woke you up nice."

"You figured right." I palmed her head, tipping her face up so I could kiss her. "Now, after all that hollerin' you did last night, what could you possibly want at five thirty in the morning?"

She laughed, but the sound was low, curling from deep in her throat. "You really want to know what I want right now?"

"Hell, yeah. I never know what's about to fall out of your mouth."

"I want to suck you off until you're feeling so good you're promising me things you know you can't actually deliver. Then I want you to set the tone for my entire day by giving me every inch of that dick you've been keeping from me the whole time you've been at RMC."

"That's...an aggressive agenda, Ms. Sutton."

"I'm an aggressive woman, Dr. Vaughn."

She rolled on top of me, then slithered down my body

until her breasts were pressed against my thighs and her mouth was just inches away from where I needed her most. The sight of her looking up at me, her fingers wrapped around the base of my shaft, made my breath catch in my throat. She was taking her sweet time, pressing soft kisses along my hip bones, letting her tongue dart out to taste me.

"You're killing me here," I choked out.

"Good," she murmured against my thigh. "I like you a little desperate."

Her tongue finally made contact, a brief flick against the head, and I couldn't stop the curse that rolled out. She smiled against me like she'd won some kind of prize, then took me into her mouth with agonizing slowness. The wet heat was enough to make my vision blur at the edges.

I tangled my fingers in her hair, not guiding her but needing something to anchor me to reality. She worked me with a patience that bordered on cruel, alternating between long, slow pulls and quick flicks of her tongue that had me fighting to stay still.

"Shit," I breathed. "You wake up in the gutter, huh?"

She pulled back just enough to speak, her lips still brushing against me. "Maybe waking up next to you brings out the nasty in me."

Her gaze held mine as she took me deeper and I had to close my eyes and concentrate on breathing. Every nerve ending in my body zeroed in on the feeling of her lips, the brush of her tongue, teeth catching gently and sending a ripple straight through me.

I tipped my head up, mesmerized by the way her cheeks hollowed, her jaw flexed, the pleasured groans that rolled from her as her lips slid up and down my length.

I couldn't take it anymore. I relaxed, let my thighs fall open, and laid a hand on either side of her neck. My base instinct took over and I began to thrust into the sweet heat of her mouth.

"Harper...Christ...the way you...I can't even..." I let out a string of curses, her name tumbling from my lips as my hips undulated, my words dissolved into a groan as she hummed around me.

Harper seemed pretty proud of herself, the way she glanced up at me—smug, like she had me right where she wanted me.

And she did. I tried to keep it together, but she was relentless. Her tongue worked magic, swirling and pressing, and she didn't let up.

"Harper...fuck! Shit, just like that."

Right when I thought I'd be shooting a load down her throat, she pulled off, aiming the stream at my chest and abs instead. The release painted my skin while my body vibrated with the force of climax.

"Good boy," she purred, sitting up to straddle my thighs and stroking me through it, milking every last drop. I gasped and cursed and chanted her name more times than was dignified.

When I finally floated back down to earth, her face hovered above mine, a grin stretching wide across her lips. She dipped in, kissed me, then drew back.

"That was even better than I imagined it would be."

I sighed, laughing. "Harper...seriously, where the hell have you been my whole life?"

She chuckled, then rolled off of me. I watched her walk away, appreciating the view of her high, round ass, her shapely legs, and the sway of her hips. I heard the tap turn on, then she came back with a warm washcloth.

She settled beside me on the bed and began to wipe away the mess we'd made. The intimacy of the gesture caught me off guard—this tender aftercare following something so raw and hungry.

I waited until she finished, then sat up, grabbing her by the wrist and pulling her toward me.

"Turn around," I said, keeping my tone gentle but firm. "Get on your hands and knees."

Her eyes went wide, pupils dilating, and a slow smile spread across her face. "Oh, we're doing this?"

"You think you can wake me up with head, then go about your day?" I guided her into position, watching as she settled on all fours, her perfect ass in the air.

She looked back at me over her shoulder, her voice raspy and full of sass. "I was hoping you'd want to participate."

"You ain't even got to worry about it."

I ran my hands over the curve of her hips, then down to take hold of her ass. She was already wet for me, ready, and when I slid my fingers between her thighs, she shuddered.

"Fuck..."

"You want this dick? Right now?" I positioned myself behind her, dragging across her opening, teasing. She tried to push back against me, but I held her hips firm, keeping her in place.

"Cole...please...stop playing and give it to me."

I eased into her slowly, watching as she dropped like a rock, forehead resting on her forearms. The angle was deeper this way, tighter, and we both groaned at the sensation.

"Shh..." I warned, beginning a nice, slow fuck. "It's too early for us to get loud."

I heard a giggle rise from her. "You think I give a fuck?" She pushed back against me, taking me deeper. "Shiiiit. You feel too good to hold back."

I tried to move slowly, just to keep the headboard from tapping the wall, but Harper had other ideas. Every time I pushed forward, she matched me, her ass bouncing back against my hips. The vision made my mouth go dry just watching her.

"Harder," she demanded, her voice muffled against the mattress.

"You sure?" I asked, not letting up but waiting for it, the confirmation.

"Cole, I fucking swear to—"

I chuckled. I liked when Harper got all frustrated and cussed at me to give her what she's been begging for. I obliged, driving into her with enough force to make her yelp. Her fingers clutched at the sheets; the sounds she made were music to my ears.

"Right there," she panted. "Don't stop! Don't you dare fucking stop."

I held steady, laser-focusing on the way her body responded to my movements, the way she pushed back to meet me, chasing her pleasure. One hand slid around to find her clit; a few tight circles later, she nearly fell apart.

"Ah! Fuck, Cole—"

"You 'bout to come?" I teased, already knowing the answer.

Harper bucked up so quick I almost lost my grip on her. Her hands flew to the headboard, gripping it like she was about to ride out a tornado. She snapped her thighs wide open, knees sinking into the mattress, and began to pulse her hips in tight little circles, grinding herself against me with unfiltered, aggressive need.

Scooting up, I grabbed her by the waist to hold her close —to be close to her. I clutched a breast in one hand, her clit in the other, and squeezed both, gentle at first, and then rougher when I heard the way she went wild. It was like I'd flipped a switch and turned her from just woke up to coming apart in half a second.

Her body told me she was close. The way her pussy pulsed around me, the way her muscles tensed, the way her teeth clenched and all of her pleas and commands came out like animalistic grunts.

I gave it to her. Hard. Fast. Deep. Skin to skin, hips slapping against her ass, the sound of our impending climax echoing off the damn walls.

So much for being quiet.

Harper rode every stroke, chasing the high, determined to get hers. When she came, there was a sharp gasp, a loud cry, and the way she clenched around me like a vise, I went down with her. I dug my fingers into her hips and pounded out another release, groaning into the pre-dawn quiet.

I stayed buried inside her as long as I could, both of us breathing hard. Finally, I eased out and she collapsed onto her side, pulling me down next to her.

"I'm gonna have to start doing some cardio," I said, still panting as I wrapped my arms around her.

She laughed. I was proud of how sated she sounded. "Was I too much at five thirty in the morning?"

"You should be that and more at all times. Wake me up like that any time you want."

She kissed my chest, her hand resting over my heart. "I do admit I like having you here. Waking up with you is nice."

"Understatement of the year, Harper."

I stroked her back, fingers exploring all of the skin I could reach. Outside, the city was starting to wake up—distant traffic, a siren somewhere far off. But in here, it was just us.

"I don't want to go to work today," Harper said quietly.

"Then don't. We could both call in, play hooky, fuck all day."

She sucked her teeth. "Right. Don't play with me, Cole."

I tucked a curl behind her ear. "When's the last time you took a day off?"

"My sister asked me that last week. I almost cussed her out."

"Sounds like you're overdue, then. Come on," I cajoled, jiggling my shoulder. "Call out."

She bit her lip, considering. "I could use a day that's not about the hospital and the Greene case."

"Sounds nice, huh?"

"You don't have to go in?" she asked, tipping her head up to see my face.

"I mean, yeah. But considering they're trying to trash my reputation, I don't really give a shit if they're mad about me taking another day. I have vacation out the ass I need to use. So..."

I shrugged, then pushed out a sigh. "I'm calling in. You're calling in too."

"Deal. I'm going to make coffee and text Rowan."

Harper rolled out of bed and padded out of the bedroom, hips swaying, not shy about it at all. I watched her go, unable to help myself. Harper wasn't the kind of woman who faded into the background. She was tall with curves that pulled your attention to the generous line of her hips, the thickness of her thighs, the way her breasts looked in a good bra.

She was lush and sensual, the kind of woman you could never get enough of.

A while later, she came back with two mugs of coffee,

steam rising from both. She'd thrown on a short silk robe that hung open, revealing everything underneath. I pushed myself up, pulling the sheets around my waist.

"Here we go." She handed me a mug and climbed back into bed, settling cross-legged beside me. "Let me know if you need cream or sugar."

I took a sip. It was quite strong. "I'm not much of a coffee drinker, but..."

"Oh." She glanced at me with a shy smile, eyes wide. "I assumed. Do you want tea? Water?"

"Nah. My baby made me some coffee, I'm going to drink it."

"Rowan picks on me about my coffee habit. I like this brand that's way too expensive, but it's all I drink at home. The blend is nice; bold but doesn't taste burnt."

"It's good. Can't say I'm a coffee drinker now, but I like that." I set my mug on the nightstand and dropped an arm around her as she tucked into me.

We sat like that for a while, drinking our coffee, talking about nothing important. It felt good. Normal. Like being a couple.

I hadn't been part of a couple in a long time, and the last time I'd been part of a couple, things didn't end up the way I'd thought they would. There was so much disappointment on both sides. I thought she understood my life. She thought I'd cut back on something I'd committed myself to for her.

Truth be told, I was scared as hell to start something with Harper. But I was even more scared to enter a future without even a possibility of a life with her.

"So," Harper said, reaching around me to set her mug down. "What are we actually going to do with this day off? Besides the obvious."

"The obvious being more sex?"

She grinned. "We should refuel. Maybe rinse off."

"Conserve water, shower with a friend?"

She rolled her eyes. "Down, boy."

"You started it at five thirty this morning." I pulled her closer. "I'm just trying to keep up."

Her laughter faded into something softer. "Last night was so good."

"Which part? The wine? Multiple plates of your mother's cooking? Drinks and after-dinner activities?"

"All of it." She looked up at me. "You being here. Talking through everything. Feeling like I'm not letting you deal with this alone."

"You're not. You're here and I know it. I feel it." I kissed the top of her head. "And those documents you put together? That's some next-level shit, Harper. You covered everything."

"Thanks. You need to send them to your attorney once you get him retained." She sat up, shivering a little and pulling her robe closed. "Your dad said he'd connect you with someone, right?"

"Yeah. Guy out of Atlanta. Dad said he's supposed to be good." I poked a finger into the opening of her robe and pried it back open.

"Cole," she chided, but she was smiling. "I'm trying to have a serious conversation about your legal situation."

"And I'm trying to see you naked." I tugged at the silk. "We can multitask."

She sighed, pretending to be exasperated, and lay back. I leaned over her, pulling both sides of the robe open just to look at her.

"The sooner he has everything, the sooner we can figure out your strategy."

"Mmmhmmm. Strategy," I repeated, tracing a finger between her breasts, then around each nipple.

"I'm in this thing, whether Rice likes it or not."

"She's going to lose her mind when she finds out I lawyered up."

Harper's laugh was cut short by the buzzing of my phone. I reached over to grab it from her nightstand, squinting at the screen. The number had an Atlanta area code.

"I think this is my dad's lawyer."

Harper sat up, pulling her robe closed. I made a face as the view of her breasts disappeared. "Answer it," she said, nodding at my phone. "Put it on speaker."

I pressed accept, switching to speaker. "Cole Vaughn here."

"Dr. Vaughn, Vincent Cross from Cross & Associates." A rich voice tinged with a Southern accent boomed through the speaker. "Walter gave me the rundown on your situation with Ridgeway Medical, said you might need a hand. I've got a gap in my trial calendar and I'm glad to help. Especially for the son of an old friend."

"Mr. Cross, hey. Thanks for calling me back." I watched Harper slide into work mode, her eyes flicking up to mine. "Just so you know, you're on speaker, and Harper Sutton is here with me. She's in Risk Management at Ridgeway."

"Ms. Sutton. Walter mentioned you'd been helpful. Good to know Dr. Vaughn has someone on the inside who understands both sides of this."

Harper leaned closer to the phone. "Thank you. I've been trying to make sure Cole—Dr. Vaughn—has everything he needs to go into this meeting next week."

"That's smart. Being prepared is going to be key here. So..." Papers rustled on his end. "Dr. Vaughn, I want to start by saying what Walter already told you. From what I understand about this case, you made the right call. My job is to make sure everyone else understands that."

"I appreciate that."

"Here's what I need from you. First, you need to officially retain my services—I'll email an engagement letter today. Once you sign it, everything we discuss is protected, so the hospital can't compel you to share our conversations."

"Got it."

"Second, I need all relevant documentation. Medical records, your surgical notes, ER intake reports, any internal communications about the case. Ms. Sutton, I understand you have a good grasp on the material?"

"Yes. I've already assembled a brief—timeline of events, protocol analysis, everything that shows Dr. Vaughn followed proper procedures."

"Excellent. Send that to my office as soon as you can. I'll review everything and we'll schedule a prep session before your meeting with the Hart family's attorney. You've met her, Ms. Sutton?"

Harper rolled her eyes. "Rachel Gaines, yes. She's based here in Ridgeway. High-profile, aggressive. She's positioning this as a grieving family looking for answers, but she's building leverage, either for a settlement or a lawsuit."

My gut clenched like a fist. Harper's fingers found my shoulder, tracing a path down my arm that seemed to say without words *I'm here, I've got you.*

I clutched her hand and offered her a smile. "So what happens next?"

"I'll fly up on Monday. We'll spend time making sure you're comfortable with your responses. No surprises, no defensive reactions. We present the facts calmly and let them speak for themselves. The fact that you're showing up with an attorney is going to send them for a loop."

"Sounds good."

"Last thing—and this is critical. No more conversations with hospital administration about this case. That includes Dr. Webb, hospital counsel, anyone except Ms. Sutton. If they try to engage you about it, decline that conversation."

"I told Cole to keep the fact that he's retained an attorney under wraps. I don't want RMC to start building a defense against Cole. They haven't come out and said they're trying to tank him, but all arrows point there. I don't want to give them any leverage."

"Good thinking, and I agree. And both of you—don't discuss this case with colleagues. If any press contact you, decline to comment. Then call me."

The word *press* hit me like a punch. "You think this case would get that kind of attention?"

"It's possible. The Hart family has money and connections. Gaines knows how to use media pressure. We're not going to let this play out in the press."

Harper nodded. "The hospital would rather keep this quiet too. Bad press hurts donations."

"Dr. Vaughn, your father tells me you're one of the best trauma surgeons in the area. I don't doubt it. You saved lives before this case, and you'll save lives after. We're going to make sure the Hart family understands that Earl Greene's death, while tragic, was not the result of negligence or a policy violation."

"Thank you, Vincent."

"You're doing the right thing by getting ahead of this. A lot of physicians wait until it's too late. Smart move. Talk soon."

"Well," Harper said after the line went silent, drawing

the word out with a wry twist of her lips, "that was good, actually. He sounds like he's done this a time or two."

"Yeah," I echoed, and felt the word as a physical relief in my chest. "And at least now we have a plan." I squeezed her hand, which was already resting in mine, our fingers locked.

"I'll send him everything today. The sooner he can review it all, the better."

"Thank you," I said. "For doing this. For putting all that together. And standing up to Dr. Rice and...last night. I mean the documents. Not the food. Or the wine. Or the sex..."

I was rambling and she was laughing at me, her whole body shaking with it.

"You're welcome for all of it," she said, pressing a kiss to my chest. "The documents, the food, the wine, and especially the sex."

"How about for, like...past the sex?" I asked.

"Like what do you mean?" she asked, tilting her head to look at me properly.

"I mean what I said. Past the sex. Friendship and dating and...learning about each other. Exclusively."

I trailed off, realizing I was venturing into territory we hadn't really mapped out yet. I didn't want to go too deep without knowing if she was ready to swim there with me.

"We can talk about that." She stood, pulling her robe open again and doing a little shimmy for my benefit, then turned toward the bathroom. "Come on, Dr. Vaughn," she called over her shoulder. "Help me conserve some water."

Deflection. She wasn't ready. And that was fine. For now.

There was an intimacy between us already that was more than sex. A personal relationship that superseded professional respect. The care we took with each other both on and off the clock had to be jarring for someone like Harper. She was risking so much to help me. And I could tell she was fighting against what her heart wanted.

We stepped into the shower together. The water ran hot, steam filling the spacious bathroom. Harper pressed her forehead against my chest while I worked conditioner through her hair and massaged her scalp.

"You're good at this," she murmured.

"These surgeon's hands are multi-talented."

When we got out, I wrapped her in a bath sheet, taking every opportunity to drop kisses on her skin. I lounged on the bed while she worked three assorted products through her curls before covering them with a silk bonnet. She let me slather her body in shea butter before pulling on a long t-shirt and leggings, then she tossed a bottle of lotion at me and went to retrieve the clothes I'd worn the night before from the dryer so I could get dressed.

After breakfast, Harper checked her email once, made a face, and set her phone on the charger on the counter. "Rowan sent me four messages. I'm ignoring all of them."

"What'd she say?"

"They. Rowan is non-binary. The first text was that they hoped I was feeling okay. Then the messages got progressively nosier. I almost never take time off, so this is odd behavior for me. The last message is a gif of Kermit the Frog drinking tea."

I laughed. "They know you well."

"Too well."

We left the dishes in the sink and migrated to the living room. Harper turned on a movie, then pulled out her laptop.

"I need to get this stuff to Vincent," she said, settling cross-legged on the couch. "Shouldn't take long."

I watched her work out of the corner of my eye, amused at the way she bit the inside of her cheek when she was reading something closely, how she'd pull up a document, scan it, mark it off on her little makeshift checklist and move on to the next document.

Organized. Methodical. Thorough. I was lucky to have her.

"You need help?" I asked at one point.

"No, I've got it. This is just tedious, and easier if I do it myself."

I pulled out my phone and tried to distract myself. Scrolled through news articles. Checked my email—three messages from the hospital I didn't open. Talia had texted, asking if I was alive. She'd called the other night but I'd been with Harper. I sent back a thumbs up and a promise to call her later.

Then I made the mistake of googling *medical malpractice lawsuit*. Big mistake. I locked my phone and set it facedown on the coffee table.

"I'm sorry. Are you bored?" Harper asked without looking up.

"Nah. I'm good. Just need to stay off the internet."

"You're not googling shit about lawsuits, are you?"

"...no."

"Cole." She finally looked at me. "Stop. You're going to spiral."

"I'm not spiraling."

"Seems like you're spiraling," she said in a sing-song voice. She closed her laptop and shifted to face me. "What'd you read?"

"Nothing. Just a lot of doctors get screwed even when they didn't do anything wrong."

"True. But you have a good attorney. And you have me, and I'm— What did you call me? A dog with a bone about this shit?"

She reached for my hand. "We're ahead of this. Most people aren't."

I squeezed her hand. "I know. Thanks."

She studied my face for another moment, then nodded and went back to her laptop. Twenty minutes later, she sent the final email and slammed the lid shut.

"Done. Vincent Cross now has everything he could need to defend you. More than he needs, but I didn't want to take chances." She stretched, arching her back. "Now I'm starving again. You hungry?"

"I'm a six foot two Black man. I can always eat. What do you feel like?"

We ordered too much Thai food and ate straight from the containers while half-watching a movie neither of us would be able to name later. Harper kept stealing bites of my curry even though she'd ordered her own dish.

"Hey! Thief!"

"Food tastes better when it's not mine."

"Got FOMO, huh? You should have ordered the curry." I shooed her fork away, frowning. "Get out my plate, woman!"

Later, after the food was gone and the sun had set and the movie had ended, Harper shifted to lay her head in my lap. She'd taken off the bonnet to let her hair air dry. I played with the soft curls that were still a little damp and enjoyed the view of the city winding down beyond her window.

"Today was so nice," she said.

I hummed my agreement. "Necessary, as a wise woman once said."

"We should play hooky more often."

I chuckled, thinking I might have all the time in the world soon.

Harper was quiet for a moment. I knew what she was going to say before she said it. "I don't want tomorrow to come."

I felt that. Tomorrow meant going back to the hospital, back to the investigation, back to pretending we weren't doing...this.

"Me either," I said. "But we gotta. Face forward, code switch on."

Chapter Fourteen

HARPER

The following Tuesday, I arrived at the conference room early. The air conditioning was running too cold, raising goosebumps on my arms beneath my navy suit jacket. My leather portfolio felt heavier than usual as I set it on the polished walnut table.

Dr. Rice stood at the window with her phone pressed to her ear. She ended her call and crossed the room. "The Hart family should be here at nine. Dr. Vaughn confirmed he's attending."

I nodded but didn't respond. What I wanted to say was that we shouldn't be feeding Cole to them, but I'd already lost that fight.

Adrienne and Gerald entered the room, followed by Dr. Webb, his tie already loosened at the collar though it wasn't yet nine in the morning.

Behind him came Diane Hart and Rachel Gaines.

Diane looked worse than she had at our first meeting. Her eyes were swollen, the skin beneath them dark and papery, her black dress hanging loose on her frame. Rachel, on the other hand, looked like she'd sharpened her teeth on the drive over. Her suit was cream with thin black pinstripes, her blouse the hue of dried blood.

"Mrs. Hart, Ms. Gaines." Dr. Rice gestured to the chairs across from us. "Dr. Vaughn should be here any moment."

They sat. Rachel opened her folio, pulled out a legal pad, clicked her pen. The sound was loud in the quiet room. The silence—the lack of small talk and polite conversation—was deafening.

I was sure Dr. Rice wanted me to play the nice hostess, stir up some chitchat. I refused. Let them be uncomfortable.

The door swung open and Cole walked in. I fought back a gasp at the sight of him, but damn. He cleaned up nice.

He wore a dark suit. Not black, the safe choice, but a deep midnight blue that made his brown skin look regal under the fluorescent lights. His shirt was crisp white, his tie a burgundy silk.

But it was the man behind him who made everyone sit up straighter.

Vincent Cross was a tall, broad dark-skinned man. He strode into the room with the energy of a man twenty years younger than his sixty-odd years. His hair was close-cropped, his deep olive three-piece suit impeccable, gold cufflinks catching every beam of light. Even his caramel-colored briefcase, worn at the edges, boasted of courtroom victories.

I could not be more excited for this moment.

Dr. Rice shot to her feet so quickly her chair rolled backward and nearly hit the wall. Rachel stood as well, a deep V forming between her brows. I was amused at the observation that her bob was slightly askew.

"Oh...uh, Cole," Dr. Rice choked out. "We weren't advised you'd be bringing counsel. We have legal representation in the room."

She gestured toward Adrienne and Gerald, whose expressions had fallen.

"I don't believe we've met," said Cole, stretching a hand to Dr. Rice and forcing her to a tenuous, stiff handshake. "Dr. Vaughn. This gentleman is Vincent Cross, of Cross & Associates."

"Good morning, Dr. Rice." Vincent's voice boomed, was rich and smooth with just enough arrogant tinge to make the moment interesting. He did not offer to shake her hand. "I'll be representing Dr. Vaughn in this matter."

"This isn't a deposition," Adrienne said. "Today is simply an opportunity for Mrs. Hart to ask Dr. Vaughn questions directly."

"Then you won't mind if I sit in." The leather sighed as Vincent sat and set his briefcase on the table.

Dr. Rice and Adrienne exchanged a look. Gerald cleared his throat.

Cole sat beside Vincent, his spine straight, his hands folded on the table. His eyes found mine for half a second. I saw the tension in his jaw, the way his shoulders were locked tight.

Rachel assessed Vincent, her gaze sweeping over him the way lawyers do when they're sizing up the opposition. "Is there a reason I wasn't informed that Dr. Vaughn would have representation? Has this meeting morphed into a legal proceeding?"

Vincent's tone stayed pleasant, but I heard the steel underneath. "The hospital has provided representation for itself. Mrs. Hart has an attorney as well. Likewise, Dr. Vaughn saw fit to engage me to protect his personal interests. Shall we begin? I'm sure we're all busy."

Rachel moved to her chair. Dr. Rice sat as well and folded her hands on the table.

"As Ms. Sutton outlined in last week's meeting, we're here to address any remaining questions Mrs. Hart has regarding her grandfather's care. Dr. Vaughn is present to provide clarity on the medical decisions made that day."

"Before we begin," Vincent said, his voice slicing through Dr. Rice's prepared statement like a scalpel through skin. "I'd like clarification. Are we here to review the facts of Mr. Greene's care? Or are we here because Ridgeway Medical Center has already decided to position my client as responsible for an outcome that was, by all medical standards, unavoidable?"

The air conditioning kicked on with a low hum.

Finally, Rachel leaned forward. "No one has accused Dr. Vaughn of anything."

"Then this should be a very short meeting," he said, with a wider smile.

Vincent opened his briefcase and pulled out a stack of documents. Paper rustled as he set them on the table.

"The facts, which have already been provided to you, are clear. Dr. Vaughn and his team followed every protocol, performed an emergency procedure in an attempt to save his life, and exhausted every option available. The outcome was tragic, but it was not the result of negligence or deviation from RMC standard of care."

"And that's fine, but the crux of the complaint was that

the family was not appropriately contacted before surgery," Rachel argued.

"The family was not reachable." Vincent didn't miss a beat. "Emergency medical protocols allow for implied consent when a patient is incapacitated and family is unavailable. Dr. Vaughn operated under those protocols. To suggest he should have waited is to suggest he should have allowed Mr. Greene to expire without intervention."

Rachel's jaw tightened. I watched a muscle jump near her temple and her face begin to flush. "One phone call? One message? That's not reasonable effort."

"It's documented effort."

Vincent slid a copy of the call log across the table. "Aside from Brookside notifying Mrs. Hart that her loved one had been transported to the hospital, the ER attempted contact. A message was left. Dr. Vaughn was informed that family could not be reached. He made the decision to proceed, which was well within policy. If you'd like to argue that was the wrong decision, I'd be happy to put that argument in front of a jury and let them decide."

Diane pressed both hands to her face. The sounds of her ragged, uneven breathing filled the spaces between words.

"Mrs. Hart," I said quietly. "Would you like—"

"My grandfather died alone." Diane's words came out halting and broken. Tears streamed down her face. "I should have been there. Someone that loved him should have been there."

"Mrs. Hart, this is an emotional time." Vincent's tone changed, the steel giving way to something softer. "Losing someone you love is painful. Feeling like you didn't get to say goodbye makes it worse. But this hospital did attempt to reach you, and Dr. Vaughn did everything possible to save your grandfather's life."

Rachel's pen started tapping again, click-click-click against her legal pad. "Be that as it may, the hospital has a responsibility—"

"The hospital has a responsibility to provide competent medical care. Which it did." Vincent sat back. "What the hospital does not have is the right to manufacture a scapegoat to make the family feel better about an outcome no one could control."

"Mr. Cross." Dr. Rice held out a hand as if to halt conversation. "No one is suggesting—"

"With respect, Dr. Rice," Vincent cut in, "that's exactly what's being suggested." He paused, letting his eyes sweep the room. "Otherwise, we wouldn't be here. This case cleared your internal post mortem review. Dr. Vaughn's surgical notes are thorough and demonstrate adherence to protocol. The ER documentation shows appropriate triage and escalation. There is no basis for a claim of negligence, and everyone in this room knows it."

Vincent let the silence stretch out, long and uncomfortable. Then he leaned forward again, his hands flat on the walnut table.

"So, let's just be clear," he continued. His wedding band glinted in the sunlight beaming through the windows. "If Ridgeway Medical Center wants to continue this narrative, positioning Dr. Vaughn as responsible for an unavoidable death to appease a donor family, let's go. But you should know that Cross & Associates is prepared to file suit against this hospital for defamation, wrongful termination if Dr. Vaughn's employment is affected in any way, and intentional infliction of emotional distress."

Gerald shifted in his seat. The leather squeaked. "That's—"

"Well within Dr. Vaughn's rights. And only the beginning." Vincent smiled, but it was all teeth. "Because when we file, the complaint will be public. We'll make sure every surgeon in this hospital knows that Ridgeway will throw its staff under the bus when money is involved. We'll make sure every potential donor knows that your institutional priorities are driven by optics, not medicine. I will make this the most expensive mistake you've ever made. By the time we're done, you'll be writing checks with so many zeros, they might as well rename this place Vaughn Medical Center."

Vincent's words practically echoed, bouncing off of the walls. I could only imagine how magnificent he would be in court. I pulled my lips in and bit the inside of my mouth to avoid smiling.

Rachel glared across the table. Her knuckles were white where she gripped her pen.

Dr. Rice was incandescently red, practically shaking in anger.

Adrienne and Gerald looked like they were doing mental math, calculating billable hours and settlement figures.

Diane Hart pressed both hands to her face. Her shoulders shook and gasping sobs filled the conference room.

"Mrs. Hart." I kept my voice low, gentle. "I'm so sorry for your loss. I know you're looking for answers, some closure. I'm just not sure that this process is going to provide the kind of comfort you're looking for."

Rachel put an arm around Diane's shoulders and helped her stand. Diane's purse fell to the floor. "We're done here," she said, bending to pick it up. "Thank you for your time."

She guided Diane toward the door. Rachel paused at the threshold, her hand on the door frame. She looked back over her shoulder, her eyes landing on Vincent.

"You'll be hearing from us."

"I'm sure we will," Vincent said, his tone as pleasant as if they'd just discussed the weekend weather.

Dr. Rice turned to Cole. Two spots of bright color remained high on her cheeks. "Dr. Vaughn, I would have appreciated advance notice of this tactic."

Cole shrugged. "And I would have appreciated the hospital not positioning me as the fall guy for a death I couldn't prevent."

"No one is positioning you—"

"Dr. Rice, let's not insult each other's intelligence."

Vincent stood, closing his briefcase with a decisive snap that made Adrienne flinch. "You expected Dr. Vaughn to show up without legal representation, hoping he'd fold and accept some form of responsibility so you don't lose a donor. You underestimated him and you underestimated me, and I take that very personally. Don't do it again."

He looked at Cole. "Got time for an early lunch before my jet takes off?"

Cole stood, buttoned his suit jacket, and followed Vincent to the door. Before he left, he glanced back at me. Our eyes met across the room and an understanding passed between us—relief, gratitude, or the acknowledgment that we'd just survived something together.

The corner of his mouth twitched as if he really wanted to bless the room with a smile. Then he was gone.

Dr. Rice turned to Adrienne and Gerald. She sighed. "Thoughts?"

"He's an arrogant piece of work, but he's not wrong," said Gerald. "If we pursue this angle, we're exposing the hospital to significant liability and publicity."

"And if the Hart family doesn't let this go?" Adrienne asked.

"Let them file," Gerald replied. "But if we throw Vaughn to them, Cross will eviscerate us."

Dr. Rice stood and gathered her things. "I need to speak with the Chairman and CEO. Let's regroup later."

She walked out without looking at me. Webb followed her.

Adrienne and Gerald packed up their briefcases and left.

I sat alone in the conference room, staring at the empty chairs, my heart still racing.

And I was delighted at the show.

* * *

I made it back to my office before Dr. Rice ambushed me.

She entered without knocking, blowing past Rowan. The door hit the wall hard enough to rattle the framed certificates. She closed it behind her with a deliberate slam.

"I need to know why you sent that man in to attack Mrs. Hart and her attorney."

I set down the pen I'd been using, clasping my hands on the desk. "I did not send anyone anywhere to do anything. I prepared materials for Dr. Vaughn to use in his defense, as per your instruction. What he did with them was his decision."

Her nostrils flared. "Don't play games with me, Harper. You knew he was bringing Vincent Cross to that meeting."

I swallowed, then quietly admitted, "Correct."

"And you didn't think that was relevant information to share with me, with Legal?"

"Dr. Vaughn's decision to retain counsel is his business, not mine. My job was to—"

Dr. Rice leaned in, slamming her palms flat on my desk. "Your job is to protect this hospital's interests. Not to arm a physician with materials to use against us."

"I didn't arm anyone with anything." I stood, my eyes meeting hers across the desk. "I provided Dr. Vaughn with the same documentation I provided to you and Legal. The timeline, the protocols, the medical justifications. Everything I prepared was factual and objective."

"You helped him build a defense."

"That is what you asked me to do, Liz. I sent those documents to you and you blessed them."

Dr. Rice stared at me. Her chest rose and fell rapidly. "You're playing a dangerous game, Ms. Sutton. From where I'm standing, it looks like you've decided to protect Dr. Vaughn at the expense of this institution."

My hands curled into fists at my sides. "From where I'm standing, it looks like this institution is trying to sacrifice a competent surgeon to appease a connected family. I will not be part of that."

Her eyes narrowed. "You don't get to make the decision about what you'll be a part of, Harper."

"Then fire me, Liz."

Dr. Rice sucked in a long breath and straightened. Smoothed down her skirt. "Excuse me?"

"If you think I'm not doing my job, if you think I'm compromised, then fire me. But I'm not going to step aside while you railroad a skilled surgeon for doing exactly what he should have done."

My pulse thrummed in my ears and her perfume was

giving me a headache as we stared at each other across my desk.

"You're walking a very thin line."

"Oh, I'm tap dancing on it."

She turned, stalking to the door in heavy, angry stomps, yanked it open, then paused. "Vincent Cross embarrassed this hospital this morning. Embarrassed me. That doesn't ever happen again. Are we clear?"

"Crystal."

The door slammed shut hard enough to make my desk lamp shake. I dropped into my chair and tried to breathe. My hands wouldn't stop trembling.

What the fuck did I just do?

My phone buzzed against the desk a few minutes later, bringing me back.

COLE:

Hey. You good? What's the mood around there?

I typed back with fingers that felt floppy.

ME:

Rice just threw a holy fit in my office.

Worth it.

COLE:

Shit. I'm sorry.

She should be coming at me, not you.

ME:

Like I said, worth it. How are you?

COLE:

Feeling good. Vincent's a beast. Gonna send my dad a bottle of something expensive to say thanks. Want to join us for lunch? We're not far.

I smiled despite everything.

ME:

He earned it. Enjoy your lunch with Vincent. I've been ignoring so much shit on my desk. Rowan will have my ass if I don't get in gear.

COLE:

Can't have that. I got plans for that ass later.

Heat crawled up my neck and my nipples tightened under my blouse. My eyes darted to the office door. Still closed.

ME:

We're flirting right now? Is that what we're doing?

COLE:

I am never gonna stop flirting with you. You sore from last night?

I grinned, my tongue slipping between my teeth as I typed while basking in the memory of the night before.

ME:

I am. In the *best* way.

COLE:

I like knowing you can still feel me. Like I left my mark.

My thighs clenched. I licked my lips and returned his message.

ME:

I cannot do this right now, Dr. Vaughn.

COLE:

You started it.

ME:

How did I start it? I was talking about work…

COLE:

You mentioned ass. Brought yours to mind. Couldn't help it.

COLE:

I have a pick-up basketball game tonight at 7 in the RMC gym. You should come watch. See what these surgeon's hands can do.

ME:

I've already experienced what those hands can do. Intimately. Had my legs shaking, body quaking.

COLE:

And I'll show you again.

ME:

Mmmmm. I hear you talking. Will you be wearing tiny, revealing shorts and a tight ass shirt?

COLE:

Maybe. You trying to see something?

ME:

Maybe.

You looked so good in your suit today. Couldn't concentrate on Vincent's threats when all I could think about was taking it off of you and getting on my knees...

COLE:

Not you reminding me about that mouth in the middle of the day in this family establishment...

ME:

You accused me of starting shit. Had to let you know what happens when I'm actually starting shit.

COLE:

Just thinking about that thing you do with your tongue.

ME:

I do a lot of things with my tongue, Cole. Which thing?

COLE:

All of them. Fuck. I need you bad right now.

I crossed my legs like that would do anything to suppress the thumping at the apex of my thighs. It did not. He was simply too good at getting me to this point with a handful of words.

ME:

Down, boy. Enjoy your lunch. I have a full day to get through.

Immediately, my screen lit up with his response.

COLE:

Yeah, take that pretty ass back to work.

COLE:

Over there being a menace in front of my salad.

Just know I'm taking you home with me tonight. We might make it through the door before I bend you over something.

My bottom lip crept between my teeth, a gasp escaping as I read his message. This was another pleasure I'd never indulged in with a lover before—most were the 'get it in and get out' type. They weren't into teasing, titillating, working up to the moment.

Cole was so good at working up to the moment.

ME:

My place is closer. In case you want to bend me over something much sooner.

COLE:

I want you in my bed. Where I won't be afraid your neighbors will pound on the wall.

I laughed at that.

ME:

My neighbors would never!

COLE:

I want to wake up with you. The way you like to wake me up.

My breath snagged in my chest. Cole did not like for me to get up and go home like I was a late-night thirst quench. He also refused to be a quick and dirty lover when he came to my home. I'd told him I had no more room on my roster and he took that personally.

I read the subtle push buried in his desires and knew there was nothing playful in his intent.

ME:

I'll come to your game. Your team better win.

COLE:

You ain't fuckin' a loser. See you later, gorgeous.

I set my phone down, my face hot, my body already humming, and it was just barely noon.

* * *

Cole was on the far side of the court in black shorts and a faded maroon Xavier t-shirt darkened with sweat. His calves flexed as he moved, staying low. When the player tried to drive left, Cole cut him off.

The ball was intercepted; Cole was already sprinting to keep up, catching a pass then pivoting on one foot. He took the shot. The ball arced through the air. I held my breath...

Swish.

"That's game!" someone shouted.

The players on Cole's team erupted. Cole's face broke into a grin when he saw me. He jogged over, grabbing a towel from the bench, his chest still heaving.

"You see that shot? Tell me you saw that shot."

I tried to keep a straight face but gave in, smiling up at him. "You think I came all the way down here to watch you miss?"

He was still catching his breath, looking at me like he

wanted to grab me and kiss me but knew better with his whole team watching. "Glad you made it."

A woman appeared beside him, wearing purple shorts and a black tank top soaked through with sweat. She glanced at me, then at Cole.

"Harper Sutton," she said slowly. "Right?"

I smiled. "That's me."

"Freida Banks, Trauma. You here to see this showboat carry this team?"

"Apparently so."

Banks grinned. "So, this is interesting."

"Freida, don't start," Cole said, but he was smiling.

"I'm just observing that Cole brought a guest to pick-up basketball. Which he has never done in the history of pick-up basketball."

One of the other players walked over—tall, built like he spent more time in the weight room than most people spent sleeping. He wore black shorts and a white tank top.

"You brought a guest to watch me play?" he asked, his voice deep and rumbling.

"Harper, this is Jackson," Cole said. "He's a fellow in plastics. And don't let his height fool you. He can't get past me."

Jackson grinned, showing perfect white teeth. "Cole should worry about not injuring himself trying to jump over me."

"Well, I'm here to watch his team win, so..."

"Oh, she's funny." Jackson elbowed Cole in the ribs. The sound was dull, meaty. "I like her."

"Ow," Cole said, flinching. "I told her I dominate this court. Play along."

"Can't. This is too good." Jackson turned to the rest of

the players, his voice carrying across the gym. "Vaughn brought a woman to watch him play basketball!"

The entire team stopped. Seven heads turned to stare.

"Are we...seriously? We're doing this?" Cole glared at Jackson, who grinned, completely unbothered.

"Absolutely," said Banks. "This is monumental."

The team erupted in laughter.

"It be your own people," Cole groaned.

They ran one more game and when it was over, Cole walked back to the bench, his shirt completely soaked now. He grabbed his water bottle and drained it before he sat beside me.

I felt the heat radiating off his body, could smell the salt and sweat. It was erotic to me.

"Verdict?" he asked, panting hard.

"You are, indeed, good with your hands."

His brows danced, eyes darkening as he leaned closer. "But you already knew that."

"Still nice to watch."

"Wait until we get home." His hand brushed my thigh, just for a second, hidden from view. "I'm gonna remind you exactly how good."

Banks walked past with her gym bag. She caught my eye and winked.

The gym was starting to empty. Someone turned off half the overhead lights.

Cole stood, offered me his hand. I took it, let him pull me up.

"Give me ten minutes to shower," he said. "Then we're out of here."

The parking deck was mostly empty by the time we left the gym. Our footsteps echoed as we walked hand in hand.

We reached my car first. I unlocked it but didn't get in and turned to face him.

"Today was a lot," I said.

"Indeed." He stepped closer. "But no matter what happens, I feel like we won."

"Vincent Cross is terrifying. Glad he's on our side."

Cole laughed. "He really is. But right now?" His hand found my waist, pulled me against him. "I'm not thinking about Vincent."

"No?"

His other hand slid up my spine. "I'm thinking about getting you out of this suit. Been thinking about it since I walked into that conference room."

"Cole..."

"I know. Down, boy." He kissed my neck, just below my ear. "The only reason you're still wearing it is because we're at work."

I shivered. His mouth moved lower, teeth grazing my collarbone through my blouse.

"You have no idea what you do to me."

My hands gripped his shirt, pulling him closer. "Tell me."

"I'd rather show you." His hand slid down, cupped my ass, squeezed hard enough to make me squeal. "I need to be with you, inside you, around you. I need you in my bed. I need to feel you come apart under me. I've been thinking about you all day and I can't take it anymore."

I kissed him. Hard. He pulled me flush against him as he backed me against the car. I felt his length, rock hard against my hip.

When I pulled back, we were both breathing like we'd just run sprints.

"I'm going to drop by my place and grab a bag."

"Don't take too long. I'll be waiting."

I got in my car and started the engine. Through the windshield, I watched Cole throw his gym bag in the back seat of his Range Rover and climb in. His headlights flicked on.

As I pulled out, I caught sight of him in my rearview mirror, following close.

We were going to celebrate. I knew exactly how and I could not wait.

Chapter Fifteen

HARPER

Dr. Rice and I had been at a cold, professional stalemate for the past few weeks. Every interaction was balanced on the razor's edge between formality and rudeness.

It was exhausting, and yet there was something perversely entertaining about it. I suspected she wanted to fire me out of spite, but if she were even tempted to try, my first call would be to Vincent Cross.

Understanding that she knew that and knew she couldn't do shit to me was delicious.

My system alerted to a new email as I'd returned from another meeting with another family with another problem, one RMC hoped I'd resolve in their favor. They were asking an awful lot of a person they couldn't count on to back up their shady head of Risk Management and Patient Advocacy.

I pulled my phone to check the email and my heart dropped into the pit of my stomach.

Subject: Hart Family Matter - Resolution

From: Rachel Gaines, Esq., Hart Legal Group

To: Dr. Elizabeth Rice, Ms. Harper Sutton

Cc: Ridgeway Medical Center Legal Department

Please be advised that the Hart family has elected to withdraw their complaint against Ridgeway Medical Center and Dr. Cole Vaughn. Mrs. Hart thanks you for your time and diligence in exploring the events surrounding the death of Mr. Earl Greene.

No further action is required at this time.

Regards,

Rachel Gaines, Esq.

Hart Legal Group

I read it twice, then a third time, waiting for the catch. There had to be a catch. Connected families like the Harts didn't just withdraw complaints, at least those with resources and influence.

My phone rang. Dr. Rice's name scrolled across the screen.

"You saw the email," she said without preamble when I picked up.

"Yes. Just now."

"I just got a call from Legal. Mrs. Hart wants to meet with you to put this to bed. Today, if possible. I've already confirmed with her attorney that this is legitimate. The complaint is being withdrawn, no conditions."

"What does she want to meet about if the complaint is going away?"

"I don't know and I don't particularly care. Schedule

the meeting, hear what she has to say, and close this file." A pause. "This is a good outcome, Harper. For everyone." Then she hung up.

Her underhanded commentary did not miss me.

I then forwarded the email to Cole with a single line: *Call me when you can.*

A text message appeared almost immediately.

COLE:

On my way to your office.

My pulse kicked up.

ME:

Now? Aren't you working?

COLE:

Be there in five.

I could have told him to wait, that this wasn't the time or place, that we needed to maintain boundaries at work, especially since the investigation was closed and we had no more excuses to see each other.

Instead, I smoothed my blouse, checked my reflection in the dark screen of my monitor, and waited.

A few minutes later, my office door opened without a knock. Cole strolled in and shut the door behind him. He wore standard dark blue scrubs and a white coat, his ID badge clipped to his chest pocket. His hair was disheveled as if he'd been running his fingers through it, but his brown eyes were smoky and he seemed...alert.

Cole was honestly rakishly handsome, standing in the middle of my office.

He crossed the room in three strides, pulled me up from my chair, and dropped his lips to mine like he had every right to—in my office, in the middle of the workday, with my door closed but not locked and the blinds only half-drawn.

When he finally pulled back, I was breathless and light-headed.

"Good morning," he said. "Missed you."

"It's been like four hours since we saw each other," I whispered. "What are you doing?"

"Kissing you." He traced his thumb across my bottom lip. "And staking my claim. Making shit real clear. I'm not hiding my feelings for you anymore."

"Cole, we're at work. We ca—"

"I know where we are." His hand slid to the small of my back, pulling me against him. "I also know I'm tired of pretending I don't want you every second of every day, no matter where we are. That I don't want everyone in this building to know you're mine."

My heart galloped double time. "Yours? Aren't we possessive, Dr. Vaughn?"

"We sure as fuck are, and I know I'm not the only one."

I bobbed my head side to side. I could admit that I'd have a severe problem if someone else laid a claim to him. I was in too deep and not asking to be rescued. "You right. So, you came all the way to my office to get a kiss and claim me?"

"I need you to let me do something."

"Oh?" A brow flicked up. "Do we need to dip to the supply closet for this?"

He scowled playfully. "Harper. It's ten in the morning. Damn."

His voice dropped lower. "I want to take you out. Make it nice. Dinner, whatever show you want to see, the whole thing. I'm done with kisses in the parking garage and fucking in a storage closet and hoping nobody sees us having dinner together. I'm done with only loving on you behind closed doors."

A month ago, I would have been adding up the consequences—the rumors, the office grapevine, what this would do to my reputation, my career. I didn't go looking for a tall, dark, handsome surgeon to bust into my life, ravage my body from head to toe on a regular basis, and make me want something I'd told myself I didn't want, hadn't wanted for a very long time...

Then Cole Vaughn came along and my life became complicated in ways I never saw coming. He became the name I couldn't get out of my head, the force I kept drifting toward without meaning to. Wanting him became a welcome feeling.

Beneath all of it, I couldn't stop myself from hoping he'd feel the same, that he'd never lose that hunger for me.

"Okay," I said.

His eyebrows rose. "Okay? That's it? No arguments?"

"I know how you love that but..." I shrugged my shoulders and grinned. "What do you want me to say? No, let's keep sneaking around? I'm grown. I want to act grown."

"Woman..." Cole shook his head, bending to kiss me again. "You are very grown. I want to make sure this is what you want."

I reached up, cupped his face in my hands, and brought his lips to mine again. "I want this. I have no idea how this dating someone from work thing goes, but I want it."

Cole's smile was devastating. "Bet. Saturday? I'll pick you up?"

"Cole—"

"Seven, Harper. Wear something that makes you feel good." He kissed me again, slower this time. "I got to run. I've been hiding from Dr. Webb. I'll see you later."

He walked out, leaving my door open behind him, and I stood there like a dreamy teenager, one hand braced on the edge of my desk, the other pressed against my mouth. I couldn't remember the last time anybody left me speechless. It wasn't a thing that happened to me.

Rowan appeared in the doorway thirty seconds later, eyebrows hiked somewhere near their hairline. "So," they said. "That was the legendary handsome Dr. Cole Vaughn."

"It was." I sighed, smiling, and went back to my chair.

Rowan grinned. "Damn, girl. Now I understand why you've been glowing."

"I'm going to need you to pretend you didn't see him kissing me, though I know you were watching because you're nosy."

"See what? Already forgotten." They turned to leave, then paused. "But if someone happens to update the RMC employee group chat, it wasn't me."

My jaw dropped. "Oh shit. Don't tell me you're on that."

"I plead the fifth. I'll just say...everyone already knows there's something going on between you two. It's all over your faces. There's a pool on when you'd go public. Pretty sure I just won a smooth hundred dollars."

"That should not be fair," I yelled as they scooted out of my office, laughing. "That's insider trading!"

* * *

I'd arranged to meet Diane Hart at two o'clock. Alone. I guided her to one of our nicer guest lounges, got her a cup of coffee, and settled next to her on the couch.

This time, things felt different. Less like a battlefield.

She sat next to me, her hands folded on her lap. She was

so small and contrite without her attorney. There was no entourage, just a woman who'd lost someone she loved.

"Thank you for meeting with me," she said. "Especially considering..."

"Of course, Mrs. Hart. I'm glad we could touch base."

She nodded, looking down at her hands. "I needed to apologize. To you and especially to Dr. Vaughn. I was angry and grieving and already feeling guilty about my grandfather. My husband, Eric—his side of the family are all attorneys. They resolve everything in a courtroom. I was upset and feeling so guilty about not being there. Eric's solution was to assign one of his attorneys to step in and it was simply the wrong choice."

"Mrs. Hart—"

"Please, let me finish." She looked up, her eyes red-rimmed but clear. "My grandfather was all I had left. My parents are both gone. His wife has been gone for some time. Over the past few years, he's become difficult to care for at home, and Brookside was the only care facility that would take him. I knew he was on borrowed time, the aneurysm was just the thing that finally took him. But I couldn't accept that. I needed it to be someone's fault. I needed there to be a villain."

I stayed quiet, letting her talk.

"Dr. Vaughn tried to save him, I understood that. But more than that..." She swallowed hard. "My grandfather would have hated what I was doing. He would have been ashamed that I was trying to destroy a good Black doctor's career because I couldn't deal with my own feelings. My own guilt."

"Guilt?"

"I was at a spa when he died, drinking champagne and eating fattening food and gossiping with rich women who have nothing better to do with their time or money. I didn't hear the phone because it wasn't even on."

Her voice cracked. "I felt terrible that I wasn't there with him in his last moments. Stephen convinced me that someone else had to be responsible. Because if it wasn't Dr. Vaughn's fault, then it was mine for not being there."

The raw and honest truth was out there, laid bare between us.

"You couldn't have known," I said quietly.

"No. But I should have been there anyway." She wiped her eyes. "I've withdrawn the complaint. And I'm writing a letter of apology to Dr. Vaughn. It won't undo what I put him through, but it's a start."

"That's very generous of you. I know he'll appreciate hearing from you."

"It's the least I can do." She stood, gathering her purse. "Thank you, Ms. Sutton. For being honest with me. For not just telling me what I wanted to hear."

After she left, I went back to my office, thinking heavily about grief and blame and the stories we tell ourselves to survive loss. Then I picked up my phone and texted Cole.

ME:

Diane Hart came by. She apologized. It's really over.

COLE:

Good. Glad we can put that to bed. Now start thinking about being in my bed on Saturday.

ME:

There are several days between now and Saturday, Dr. Vaughn. Do you intend to abandon me and my needs during this time?

COLE:

Not at all. Supply closet. Ten minutes.

I let out a snort of a laugh, but then texted back.

ME:

Really? Cause...we can do that...

COLE:

I'm just playing.

Unless you're gonna do it

* * *

The weather was so perfect on Saturday, it seemed to draw everyone out and into the light. I spent the morning watching my niece play soccer, then took her and Alicia to lunch before heading home to finish some deep cleaning.

Hours later, I stood in front of my closet, discarding outfit after outfit until I settled on a deep red wrap dress that clung to me in all the ways I loved.

I lost myself in the ritual of getting ready for a date—something I hadn't done in what felt like years. Jeremiah and I didn't have nice dates. We met for meals or a show, but the main event was always a few hours of raucous sex with no emotion, no care, no yearning.

No love.

Tonight, I was excited to curl and coax my hair, apply makeup, enhance every part of my body that I knew Cole liked to explore.

Cole arrived right on time in dark slacks and a button-up shirt, no tie, the top button undone. His eyes traveled over me slowly, appreciatively.

"Amazing," he said. "I'm so happy to see you."

"Could say the same about you."

We dined at Augustine, a downtown restaurant with romantic lighting, light Southern fare, and exceptional wine. We sat at a corner table, knees touching under the tablecloth, chatting about everything except work.

It was easy. Comfortable. Like we'd been doing this forever.

After dinner, we walked to the Fox Theatre for a show —a musical I'd mentioned in passing that I'd love to see. He remembered. He held my hand in his lap the entire time, his thumb stroking my skin.

During intermission, we stood in the crowded lobby drinking overpriced wine from plastic cups when I saw him.

Jeremiah.

He was across the room with a woman I didn't recognize. She was petite, beautiful, bright red lips open wide and laughing at something he'd said. She touched his arm, casual and comfortable, and he smiled down at her like she was the only person in the building.

Cole followed my gaze. "Ain't that your boy?" he asked, clearly amused.

"Mmmmm," I hummed in confirmation.

"You want to go say hi? You want to hide?"

I turned back to Cole, surprised by how much I meant it when I said, "I don't want to do either. I'd much rather be hugged up with a surgeon nigga from my job."

We both laughed, but after another glance at Jeremiah, I never thought of him again. I didn't feel regret or loss or even curiosity. I felt relief. He'd found someone who wanted what he could give. And I'd found someone who gave without me having to ask, who showed up when it mattered, who looked at me like I was everything he'd wished for.

Cole tucked a lock of hair behind my ear, then dropped a kiss there. "You good?"

"I'm perfect," I said, leaning in for a longer, deeper kiss.

After the show, we ended up back at his place. We liked my condo, but he had so much more room. And he had Ms. Patricia, who, after learning that I existed, started leaving meals for two and decadent desserts for us to enjoy.

Cole unlocked the door and pulled me inside, his hands already reaching for me. "I've been waiting all night to get you alone," he said against my mouth.

"You had me alone at dinner."

"Not alone enough."

He walked me backward to the stairs, kissing me between steps, his hands mapping the curves of my body through the dress. He pulled me up the steps and to the bedroom, where he turned on one lamp, filling the room with low golden light.

He shrugged out of his jacket, tossed it over a chair. "Let me know if you've got somewhere to be. I plan to take my time with you."

"I'm all yours," I replied.

"Yeah? For how long?"

"How long do you want me?"

"That is actually a perfect question to ask."

He undressed me slowly, his hands reverent, his mouth following the path of each revealed inch of skin. When I was finally naked, he looked at me like I was something so precious. The look in his eyes made me want to cry.

"You're so beautiful," he whispered. "So made just for me."

"Cole—"

"Let me—I had this all planned out," he said. "Let me say it. You're beautiful and brilliant and stubborn and funny. You consume me in the best possible way. I'm so fucking in love with you, Harper. I need you to know that."

I pulled him down to the bed, needing him closer. He stripped quickly, then covered my body with his. When he finally pushed inside me, I sucked in a breath, my eyes closed. He just felt so good. So right.

"You okay?" he asked, his hips stilling.

"I am..." My eyes opened. Then I realized they were brimming with tears. "I'm more than okay."

He moved slowly, building rhythm and searing heat. Our fingers intertwined, his forehead pressed to mine, our bodies moving in sync.

"Baby," he groaned, shuddering. "Why do you feel so good right now?"

I wrapped my legs around his hips, pulling him closer, drawing him deeper. "Do not ever stop, Cole."

He shifted his angle and suddenly, he was hitting a pleasure center that made me cry out. The orgasm unfurled slow and devastating, flames licking through my body, consuming me in waves that built and built until I was on fire. When it finally crashed over me, I screamed his name, my fingers digging into his shoulders for dear life.

Cole followed seconds later, a low moan tearing from his throat as he buried himself deep.

"Stay," he said when he caught his breath. Still inside me, still on top of me, my limbs still tight around him.

"I was planning on it," I said. I was tired of pretending I wanted to get up and go home right after sex anyway.

"No, I mean...stay. With me. Let's do this. For serious, for real, forever. I meant what I said, Harper. I'm in love with you."

I tried to speak, but nothing came out except a whimper. Or a squeak. Cole laughed and kissed me again, slow and deep, his hands on my face like he needed to hold me in place.

"You don't have to say it back if you're not ready," he whispered, his lips skimming my cheek, my jaw, my neck. "I just need you to know."

"No...Cole. I—"

I didn't know what I thought would happen when I opened my mouth, but I was not prepared for the torrent of emotion that came from simply trying to tell this man I was in love with him.

Had *been* in love with him.

Was so scared of opening my heart and life to someone, but I couldn't help but fall hard for him.

Cole rolled us so he could hold me, rubbing my arms and whispering to me while I got myself together. It took a minute, pressed under his warmth and muscle like the best weighted blanket.

Then I propped myself up on one elbow, looking down at him in the dim light. His expression was open, vulnerable.

"It scares the shit out of me to say this," I said, the words tumbling out before fear could clamp down on them. "But I can't even picture my life anymore without you in it. I want this. All of it. Whatever's next, however messy or weird or sideways it gets. I want you. I want to love you. And I want you to love me back."

Cole pulled me down to him, kissing my lips. "Good. Because I'm already there."

Epilogue

COLE

Nine months later

I woke up to Harper's feet pressed against my calves.

"Babe!" I grumbled, still half-asleep. "Your feet are ice."

"Then warm them up," she said, rolling over, then scooting closer until she was pressed up against my side with her head on my chest. She slung one leg over me, her thigh slotting right between mine in a way that was not conducive to staying asleep.

I cracked one eye open. Sunlight filtered through the blinds, and a quick glance at the clock on the nightstand confirmed it was past seven. But it was my day off. No surgeries. No rounds. No residents.

Just me, this woman I fell in love with, and no reason to leave the bed any time soon.

A shrill beep cut through the peace of the morning. Harper made a whimpering sound, reaching over me to the nightstand. She grabbed her phone to silence it, then returned her head to its preferred place of rest—my chest.

"We have no plans this morning. Why did you set an alarm for nothing?" I asked her, dropping a kiss on her forehead while my palm wandered the slope of her hip beneath the blanket.

"Not nothing. I want to get some unpacking done." She tucked her face deeper into the hollow between my neck and shoulder, planting sweet kisses on my skin. "And eventually, we have to make it over to my parents' for dinner."

I raked my hand over her silk sleep scarf, massaging her scalp through the fabric with an absent-minded tenderness. "Mmmmm," I said, "but how about just having sex all morning?"

"Tempting, but Ms. Patricia is already grumpy about the boxes that have been sitting around."

It had only been a few weeks since Harper moved out of her condo in preparation to put it up for sale, but it had been a busy time at RMC and neither of us had the hours or the energy to deal with her belongings. She'd started moving in gradually—a toothbrush propped next to mine, a few pairs of soft socks rolled into my dresser.

Clothes she wore to my place were washed and put away in my closet instead of returned to hers. When the scarf she wore to bed was draped over the bathroom doorknob, I knew there was no turning back.

The guest room had become a forest of half-unpacked boxes stacked chest-high. I personally loved the chaos if it meant I had Harper with me day in and day out.

Ms. Patricia, on the other hand, was serious about getting Harper settled and feeling at home.

"So, you getting up, then?"

"Five more minutes," she mumbled.

"You said that yesterday."

"I know you aren't complaining, Cole."

"Nope, I'm not. Because we were *productive*."

She lifted her head, one eyebrow raised. "That's what we're calling it?"

"You came twice."

She swatted my chest, laughing. "You're ridiculous."

"But did I lie? And you love that about me. Ever since you were a little girl, you wanted to love a ridiculous man."

"I really did." She kissed me, slow and lazy, then sat up with a sigh. "And I really do love you."

"Love you too, morning breath. So what time do we need to be at the house?"

"Mom wants you there by one o'clock to help cook."

"So we leave at twelve thirty."

"Thereabouts."

"Good." I pulled her back down against my chest. "Then we have time to celebrate new developments in our lives properly."

She tipped her head up. "Haven't we been celebrating?"

"Not enough for a new address *and* a promotion." I pressed my lips to her temple.

She was quiet for a second, then said, "My family's going to be so extra today. They've been like this ever since I started bringing you to Sunday dinner."

"Good. Let them be extra about you." I pinched her chin, tilting her face up so I could look her in the eye. "You earned this, baby. Now is not the time to be shy about good things happening for you."

"I'm not being shy. It just feels like it took forever between the announcement that Liz was leaving RMC and when they officially promoted me to Vice President—"

"You mean when you chased her out of the hospital and took her job?"

She laughed. "That is not what happened, Cole."

"That's how I'm gonna tell it to our kids."

The Greene case was still sending aftershocks through Ridgeway. According to hallway gossip and the RMC group chat, the hospital CEO was displeased with Dr. Rice's handling of the inquiry. Bringing the institution into Vincent Cross's orbit and risking a valued member of the surgical team over a donor who barely made a blip on the fundraising radar was evidently not what the board meant by *deal with this issue.*

Dr. Rice was offered a generous separation package. She'd already lined up her next role at a hospital near Stanford University.

"She actually came to find me before she packed up her office," said Harper. "I think she expected me to make departure easy for her."

"And did you?"

Harper gave me a look that told the whole story. "About as easy as she made it for me to work with her."

She folded her hands together with a satisfied smirk on her thick, pretty lips. "She said she hoped I understood what I was walking into. That the job was harder than it looked. Then she wished me luck."

"In that way where she didn't really mean good luck."

"In exactly that way." Harper tilted her head up so her eyes met mine. "I thanked her and told her Stanford was lucky to have her."

"In that way where you didn't really mean lucky."

"Stanford *is* lucky to have her. Far away from me and my hospital." Harper bit her lip, then allowed a proud grin to spread. "Vice President of Risk Management and Patient Advocacy *is* kind of a big deal, isn't it?"

"Kind of a big title. Kind of a big paycheck. Kind of a big corner office on the Admin floor."

Harper gasped, shooting up, hissing as she lurched toward her phone. "Shit! I needed to make sure Rowan ordered a few things for my new office. They're moving us tomorrow—"

I caught her by the waist before she could tumble off the mattress, rolling her so I was on top. "Baby, it's Sunday. Leave them alone. Besides, I thought we were celebrating."

"I'll forget. I'm going to just text them."

She half-twisted in my grip, reaching for her phone on the nightstand with one hand, swatting my hands away with the other. Sleep scarf slipping to the side, face set in determined concentration. She was the world's most beautiful workaholic.

"You done?" I asked, snatching the device from her hands and tossing it to the other side of the nightstand.

"Yes," she answered, flopping back as if out of breath. "If they don't enter the supply request first thing, it'll get kicked to next week and I want them this week."

She sighed, finally relaxing again. I was close enough to kiss her...but didn't. Instead, I leaned on one elbow, dragging the sheet down so I could get a better look at her nude form. I wasn't mad at the view.

Harper flashed me a suspicious look. I almost never delayed a session of morning sex.

"What?" she asked.

"Nothing. Just thinking."

"About?"

"Dr. Webb, actually," I answered, after a few moments of hesitation.

She cringed, frowning. "You're in bed with me on a Sunday morning? Thinking about that man who couldn't even have your back when your ass was on the line?"

"It's just...we were talking about Dr. Rice and I remembered that he called me Friday. He wanted to tell me about his decision to retire."

Harper gasped and started to sit up, moving so rapidly that it threw me off of her. She propped herself up so we were face to face. "You thought he might. He's doing it, then?"

I bobbed my head in a nod. "End of the quarter."

"Did he ask you to take over as department chair?"

"He mentioned it. He said he has a lot of pull in who RMC chooses."

"And?"

"And..." I paused, bobbing my head. "I turned him down."

Harper went still, almost holding her breath. "Cole. That's—"

"I know. I know it would be—"

"—the job you've been working toward your whole career."

"I thought that's what I was working toward. What I wanted out of this whole move to this region, this job at this hospital. Turns out that's not what I want."

"Okay. News to me," she replied. "What do you want, then?"

I reached for her, tugging her closer. "Well, this, mostly. But you know what I did last Thursday?"

She shook her head.

"I spent six hours in the OR with a nineteen-year-old

kid. Motorcycle accident. Ruptured spleen, liver laceration, massive internal bleeding. Real touch-and-go type situation."

"Oh. Did he make it?"

"We pulled it off. Kid's hanging out in ICU, but he's alive. I was there, doing what I'm trained to do. What I love to do."

"So you're choosing surgery."

"I'm choosing to do the work I love instead of managing people who do the work I love. Webb spent years climbing that ladder. Now he's retiring because he's burned out and tired and he can't remember why he wanted to be at that level in the first place."

I shook my head. "I know a lot of people want that for me, but I don't want that for me."

"What did he say when you told him no?"

"That I was making a mistake. That I'd regret not taking this opportunity to guide the next generation. I think I can guide the next generation better on this side of the table."

"Do you think you will? Regret turning it down?"

I let the question hang for a minute, actually pondered it, because my answer to Dr. Webb had been quick, a knee-jerk response.

"Honestly? I don't think so. Webb didn't support me like I thought he should. He chose hospital politics over doing the right thing. I'm not interested in becoming that version of a leader."

Harper was contemplative for a moment. Then she said, "I almost turned down the VP appointment."

I pulled back to look at her. "What?"

"When they first offered it to me, I thought about saying no." She bit her lip. "It felt like they were promoting me to make themselves feel better about what happened between me and Dr. Rice. And to keep me from calling Vincent Cross, honestly. It felt like a ploy to cover their asses, create better optics."

"But you took it," I reminded her, eyes wide. "Because you deserve that appointment."

"They can give me the job for whatever reason they want, but I'm going to do the job the best way I know how for the right reasons. I can make sure no other staff member feels like this hospital doesn't have their back. I can protect people instead of protecting the hospital's reputation. And I can be a guiding light to young Black medical professionals coming up through the system."

I grinned, beaming with pride. "That's an aggressive agenda, Ms. Sutton."

Harper scooted closer, tucking herself in under my arm. "I'm an aggressive woman, Dr. Vaughn. We're both stubborn as hell, you know that?"

"Oh, yeah," I replied. "It's why we work so well. We're not in the habit of backing down from doing the right thing."

"Quiet as it's kept, we don't back down from doing each other, either."

"And neither of us are kept quiet. That's exactly why I moved you to this house."

Harper laughed, then kissed with her whole soul, like she was trying to memorize my very being. I groaned, slipping a hand up the inside of her thigh. She was already wet and so, so warm it made my dick twitch.

I teased her, running my fingers over her clit, back and forth, slow and hypnotic. Harper whimpered a tight little sound, barely there, like she was trying to hold it in but it escaped.

She hated being teased. But *loved* being teased.

I slid one finger, then two inside her and fucked her slow until she began to buck in rhythm to my strokes. She pushed out a loud, sensual hiss as her hips rolled in time.

"You shouldn't start shit you don't plan to finish," she whispered.

"We just talked about not backing down. I'm not that type of guy. Besides," I said, rolling us over so she was pinned beneath me, legs spread and ready. I positioned myself, heaving a relieved sigh as I entered her, like it was the first time I'd ever entered her. "I said we're not done celebrating."

We languished in the bed, reveling in the sound, touch, and taste of each other until we had both come completely undone and then some. I was still breathing heavy when Harper took advantage of my sated state and flipped me over onto my back.

I laughed as she straddled me. This woman was something else. A dream come true for real.

Later, we'd get up, pick through some boxes, put more of her things away. We'd shower and dress and drive to her parents' home for Sunday dinner, where her mother had become accustomed to bossing me around her kitchen. We'd eat too much and laugh too loud, then drive home with leftovers we couldn't refuse. We'd have a glass of wine and something sweet Ms. Patricia had left for us.

Then fall into bed and do what we did for each other better than anyone.

And it would be exactly what we'd almost run away from but couldn't deny.

Love.

Acknowledgments

As always, thank you to my seasoned readers, my ride-or-dies, the ones who show up every time I release a book. Your support makes it possible for me to be an author. I don't take your support for granted.

Welcome to any new readers I may have gained! Thank you for taking a chance on me and this story. I hope you enjoyed meeting Harper and Cole and spending time inside Ridgeway Medical Center. This story was fun to write.

This book pushed me in new ways, and I didn't do it alone. Thank you to my beta readers, especially those with medical experience, who helped me bring accuracy to the page. Your feedback made this story stronger, and made sure I don't look like a fool. Readers may never fully see what you all do, but I do.

To my ARC team, fellow authors, writing pals and my circle of family and friends: **thank you** for your constant and continued support, your honesty, and for holding me steady when I needed it.

Special thanks to **AdotK Edits** for a professional editing touch. I never fear the edit!

Reading Group Guide

The questions below are for readers who have finished *Standard of Care* and want to dig deeper.

1. Dr. Rice assigns Harper to Cole's investigation assuming her racial solidarity will smooth things over. Did Harper handle that the right way? What were her real options?
2. Cole walks into his first meeting with Harper expecting to be sacrificed. For Black professionals, that expectation isn't paranoia. What did Harper do to earn his trust, and when did you notice it shift?
3. Harper keeps her professional and personal lives separate. For a Black woman in senior administration, that separation can often be survival. What did it cost her ? Have you had to make the same moves in your career?
4. Both Harper and Cole lead with competence before anything else. For two people who have had to be excellent just to be taken seriously, talk about what it means to finally be seen by someone who understands that labor?
5. Diane Hart is a Black woman whose grief gets weaponized into a legal strategy, aimed at a Black doctor. How did your feelings about her shift over the course of the book?
6. Harper stays in the investigation longer than she should, risking her own career to push back against Dr. Rice. Was her choice noble or reckless?

7. Cole's father tells him to walk in with his head up and not apologize for saving lives. There's a particular kind of coaching Black fathers give Black sons about surviving institutions. How much of Cole's strength in the second half of the book comes from that conversation vs the support he's getting from Harper?
8. There's no third act breakup in this book (YAY!) Instead, it's an external threat that Harper and Cole face together. What does it say that the greatest danger to this relationship wasn't their own fears, but the institution itself?
9. Harper and Cole have every professional reason to keep their distance and choose each other anyway. At what point did you stop believing they could resist it. And did you want them to?
10. What does the title *Standard of Care* mean to you by the end of the novel?

If your book club reads Standard of Care, I'd love to hear about it. Find me at booksbydlwhite.com.

Also by DL White

Browse Books & Merch at Booksbydlwhite.com/shop

Ruby's

Brunch at Ruby's

Dinner at Sam's

Drinks at Minks, a Ruby's Companion Novella

Black Diamond Bay

Beach Thing, a Black Diamond Vacation Romance

Elysium, a Black Diamond Vacation Romance

The Pearl at Black Diamond, a Black Diamond Workplace Romance

Potter Lake Small Town Romance

Leslie's Curl & Dye

Second Time Around (Potter Lake Holiday Novella)

The Guy Next Door

Home for the Holidays (A Potter Lake Holiday Novella)

Stand-alone Novels/Novellas/Shorts

A Thin Line

The Never List

Hey, Lover, a Second Chance Romance

Olympia's on King Street (newsletter exclusive)

Baking Bad, a Sweet Crumbs Mystery

Calculated Risk (*only available in print until Sept 2025*)

Missing Persons, a Young Investigations novel

Holiday Novellas

The Kwanzaa Brunch

Unexpected

The Festival at Evergreen Falls

Grumpy Valentine

Clover (website exclusive)

Anonymous (permafree!)

About the author

DL White is an Atlanta based author of snarky, steamy, seasoned Black fiction, often centered on complicated women and the men who fall hard for them. DL is the author of more than twenty novels and novellas across multiple series and the host of ***The Bookcast,*** where she talks reading life, writing process, and what she's working on next.

New to **Books by DL White**?

• The **Potter Lake series** will feel like home. Start at *Leslie's Curl & Dye* (it's free in eBook and audio!)

• Take a trip to **Black Diamond-** Book 1 is *Beach Thing*, a dreamy romance featuring a celebrity music producer and an island woman with thick thighs and a life she loves

• Pull up a chair at **Ruby's Soul food cafe** and meet my favorites, Deborah, Maxine and Renee in *Brunch at Ruby's*.

• My standalone titles lean emotional, steamy and only a little messy. ***Missing Persons, Calculated Risk*** and ***The Never List*** are good places to start.

Browse and buy my books at **Payhip.com/Booksbydlwhite.**

www.ingramcontent.com/pod-product-compliance
Lightning Source LLC
LaVergne TN
LVHW100524110826
845146LV00002B/762
* 9 7 9 8 9 9 6 0 3 0 4 1 5 *